"Go, Tigers! Bu...

The chant spread quickly around the circle.

"Back five paces!" Coach Murphy bellowed.

We all obediently moved back across the wet grass.

A hush fell over the crowd as the cheerleaders formed a circle around the tall tower. They lowered their torches and set the pile ablaze on all sides at once.

A cheer rose up over the field as the wood flamed up. . . . Big tufts of straw lit up, tossing in the wind.

The fire shot up the tall structure, rising like a rocket, crackling, popping, darting out in all directions.

"It's beautiful!" Dana declared, slapping me a hard high five.

I had to agree with her. It looked like some kind of movie special effects.

And just as I thought that, I saw the tower start to tilt.

My mouth dropped open as the tower bent . . . bent . . . then toppled over.

I pressed my hands to my face, unable to scream.

With a rumble that sounded like thunder, the flaming straw and boards and chairs and chunks of wood came falling, falling over everyone. . . .

DON'T MISS A SINGLE NIGHT

Moonlight Secrets

Midnight Games

Darkest Dawn

FEAR STREET NIGHTS
DARKEST DAWN

R.L. STINE

SIMON AND SCHUSTER

SIMON AND SCHUSTER

First published in Great Britain in 2006 by Simon & Schuster UK Ltd.
A Viacom Company
Africa House, 64-78 Kingsway, London WC2B 6AH

Originally published in the USA in 2005 by Simon Pulse,
an imprint of Simon & Schuster Children's Division, New York.

 A Parachute Press book

Copyright © 2005 by Parachute Publishing, L.L.C.
Cover design by blacksheep-uk.com
Cover photograph © Getty Images

A CIP catalogue record for this book is
available from the British Library

ISBN 1-416-90414-X

1 3 5 7 9 10 8 6 4 2

Printed by Cox & Wyman Ltd, Reading, Berks

PROLOGUE

1

"I can't believe we're going to a Valentine's dance," Dana Fear said, shaking out her dark hair, studying herself in the dresser mirror. "It's so totally geeky."

"It's for a good cause," Jamie Richards replied. "You know all the money goes to the homeless."

"Clark knows the DJ," Dana said. "He does the mixes at that teen dance club on Wayland Road that no one goes to."

"Never been there," Jamie said. "Hey, you and Clark are together a lot these days."

Dana smoothed lip gloss over her lips. "He's hot," she murmured. "And yeah, I think he's really into me."

I was watching the two girls from the bedroom window. It was open a crack, and I could hear every word they said. They didn't see me—otherwise they would have quickly shooed me away.

Or maybe they'd scream in fright.

Pressing against the window glass, I watched Jamie slip on a sheer, violet midriff top and straighten it over her waist. "Is this too sexy?"

Dana snickered. "Too sexy? What does that mean?"

"No. Really." Jamie bumped her cousin away from the mirror.

"I like that skirt," Dana said. "It's so short. You can't sit down in it. Where'd you get it?"

"Old Navy. Believe it?"

Dana wore a loose-fitting silvery top and low-riding jeans. She wasn't as knockout pretty as her cousin Jamie, but she knew how to show off what she had.

Watching her, I felt bad that I'd made the decision to kill her.

"When is Lewis picking us up?" Dana asked.

Jamie glanced at her bedtable clock. "In half an hour, I guess. I'll call his cell and see if he's ready to leave."

Dana giggled. "This is so retro. A double date. Like in an old sitcom or something. We should have made the guys bring us corsages."

"Corsages?" Jamie frowned. "*No way* they'd know what corsages are."

I was getting bored. Also, the girls were enjoying themselves too much. We can't have that—can we?

I decided to show them I was there.

Jamie bumped Dana away from the mirror again. "I hate my hair," she said, tugging it with both hands. "Here. Help me put it up."

Dana combed her fingers through Jamie's hair. "Your hair is so much thicker than mine," she said. "And bouncier. Mine just lies there limp."

Jamie handed her the brush. "Hurry. We don't have much time."

Dana raised the brush to the back of Jamie's hair—then stopped. "Whoa. Hold on. There's something in your hair."

She pinched her fingers around the little crawling thing in Jamie's hair, pulled it out, and examined it. "Oh, my god! It's a little white worm!"

"Huh?" Jamie spun around. "Let me see it." She squinted at Dana's hand. "It's . . . I think it's a maggot!"

"Here's another one," Dana said, lifting something off Jamie's scalp. "Oh, wow. Another one. Yikes! Jamie—there are *dozens* of them!"

Dana held up four or five maggots in the palm of her hand.

"Ohh . . . my head—it *itches*!" Jamie cried, scratching frantically.

Dana ran the brush through Jamie's hair and watched the tiny white worms fall to the floor.

Jamie let out a scream. "Dana—they're in *your* hair too! Get that one! It's crawling down your forehead!"

Dana slapped at her forehead. She started frantically picking maggots from her hair.

"My scalp! It itches! It burns! Ow! We're covered in them. Covered in maggots!"

2

Both girls were screaming now, screaming and crying, and frantically pulling at their hair.

They probably wouldn't make it to the dance.

I decided it was time for me to leave. I raised my wings and took off, floating high above Jamie's house.

They still hadn't seen me. If they had, they would have screamed some more. They would have recognized me, the blackbird with one eye missing.

And they would know that the EVIL lives, the evil still haunts them.

At least, they consider me evil. I have a different point of view. I think I'm on the side of justice. I only want what is fair.

After all, they invaded my house last year. They broke into the Fear Mansion and looted it. They gleefully stole our possessions.

Didn't anyone ever teach these kids that crime doesn't pay?

Well, that's what I plan to do. I plan to teach them that important lesson.

Dana and Jamie think they have killed the evil. Burned it in that fiery kiln in Jamie's garage. They think they can relax now.

But I'm still here.

I'm closer to them than ever.

And I have the amulet. The jeweled pendant that gives me so much power.

They won't get away with their crime. I'll see to that.

I'm not evil. What an ugly word that is. I desire only *justice*.

Trying to burn us away gives me even more reason to seek my revenge.

Even more reason to kill them one by one.

PART ONE
ONE MONTH LATER

3

"Lewis, you are evil," I said. I gave him a hard shove.

He grabbed my hands and pulled me down the hall. "Check it out," he said. "My new room. Jamie, this house is so huge, it's like I have my own apartment. My parents will never even know we're in here."

"You have a dirty mind," I said. I grinned at him. "I *like* that!"

Shark and Nikki laughed. Dana dropped onto the black bedspread and pulled Clark down beside her. "What's up with the dark walls? Everything is black in here," she said, gazing around.

Lewis smiled at me. "I was watching this cable show about famous bachelor pads," he said. "These guys all had black walls. Totally cool, right?"

"But you need a mirror on the ceiling," Clark said.

We all laughed.

"Get up," Lewis told Dana and Clark. "You gotta check out the den." He trotted down the long, carpeted hall, and we hurried to keep up with him. Everything looked so bright and clean. The house still had that new-paint smell.

"Check it out," Lewis declared, waving us into the den. He clicked on the ceiling lights. We stared at the wide-screen TV on the wall. "It's plasma," he said. "We get about twenty high-def stations."

"Awesome!" Shark exclaimed. "Just in time for March Madness. Are the basketball games in high def?"

"For sure," Lewis said. "You guys can come over next Saturday and watch. You bring some six-packs. I'll get sub sandwiches. My parents are going out, so we'll have the whole house to ourselves. Par-tee!"

"Sweet!" Shark declared. He smoothed his

hand over the back of the green leather couch. "Is this real imitation plastic?"

"Ha–ha." Lewis rolled his eyes. "Sit down on it. It's so soft, you sink in about two feet."

Nikki and Dana raced to try out the couch.

"Whoa. Wait. You guys can't come here next Saturday," Clark said, waving his hands. "You've gotta come to *my* game. If we win Saturday night against Riverview, Shadyside goes to the state finals."

My cousin Dana jumped up and slid an arm around her new boyfriend's shoulders. "Yeah. We've gotta go to Clark's game," she said. "Go, Tigers—right? Shadyside rules!"

Shark laughed. "Can you picture Dana as a cheerleader?" He did a glum-faced, dull-voiced cheer. *"Go, Tigers. Go Tigers. Whatever."* A perfect imitation of Dana.

Everyone laughed except Dana. "I don't get it," she said. "I don't sound like that. I'm totally *excited* we might go to the tournament. Mainly, I like to watch Clark play."

"She likes it when Clark gets all sweaty," Shark said.

That got a big laugh. Dana gave Shark a hard slap on the back.

I stood in the doorway, watching Lewis. It made me feel good to see him smiling and happy and excited.

Things are going so well for Lewis. One, his parents bought this enormous new house. Two, he got early acceptance at Brown. So he didn't have to wait, biting his nails for the college acceptance letters in April.

Even I was starting to relax a little, starting to feel as if I could breathe normally again.

Senior year began so tragically for all of us. Three girls in our class died in the most horrible ways.

When school opened in September, I was still recovering from a painful accident. Late one night, Lewis and I fell. We were in the yard of the old Fear Mansion on Fear Street. We were curious about the ghosts and legends of the place. Everyone in town believed it to be a place of evil. Everyone believed the Fear family to be sorcerers, users of dark magic.

Anyway, the old mansion had just been torn down. Lewis and I shouldn't have been there so late at night. We fell into a deep excavation hole. We were both nearly buried. We broke a lot of bones.

It took months for us to recover. Lewis and I had to repeat senior year. When school started the following September, I still had a bad limp. The nerves in my hip and legs hadn't healed.

But I had a much worse problem, a problem I had no way of discovering. You see, the excavation where I fell had uncovered an old grave. The grave of Angelica Fear.

Angelica was said to be the most evil of all the Fears. According to the stories, she had been given an amulet—a silver, jeweled pendant with evil powers. The amulet held the secret of immortality. And before she died—a hundred years ago—Angelica swore she would come back someday.

I know it sounds totally bizarre. Totally unbelievable. But sadly, it's all true. When I fell on Angelica's grave, she rose up and possessed me. She took my body. And she used it to . . . to . . . murder the three girls in my class.

I don't know why she did it.

I don't remember any of this. I guess I'm lucky that I don't remember it. If I did, I'd probably go stark-raving nuts.

Sometimes I think I *am* crazy. Sometimes I think none of it could be true. But when I see those empty seats in homeroom, I know it happened. And there's nothing I can do about it.

My cousin, Dana Fear, came to live with me and my family in September. Her mother died, and her dad didn't want to take care of her.

Dana told me all this. Dana explained to me about how Angelica Fear took over my body, possessed me, and used me for her evil.

I had no memory of that whole time. Dana told me how she destroyed Angelica. She shoved her into the big pottery kiln in my garage. She heard Angelica's screams and watched her evaporate into a green gas.

Yes, Dana killed Angelica. She freed me from her evil ghost. I was me again. But it took so long to feel like me. It took so long to believe the horrifying story. And to believe that Angelica was gone for good.

But here we were. March. And things were

going really well for everyone. Lewis so happy. And Dana starting to get over her father's rejection. And finding Clark, a new guy she really likes.

For three months, I've been ME again. It seems that Lewis and I can finally enjoy our last months of high school and look ahead to happy times after that.

Lewis and I have been together for so long. My parents say we're like an old married couple. They say we even *fight* like an old married couple.

I don't think that's true.

In fact, things have been so strange, sometimes I'm not even sure I know Lewis that well. Sure, we see each other every day. And we still care about each other a lot. And I enjoy holding him, being with him.

But . . . there are many things we don't talk about. So many things we *can't* talk about.

So much pain and horror to cover up, I guess.

Sometimes I feel there's like a wall between us. And I wonder what he's thinking about.

Does he think about me being possessed by a hundred-year-old ghost? Does that gross him out? Does he think I'm a murderer?

Besides Dana, Lewis is the only one who knows my secret. The only one who knows the truth.

He has been very kind and very caring since . . . since it all happened. But . . . something has changed between us. It's hard to describe. I just feel a *distance* I didn't feel before.

A wall.

But maybe that is all in my mind. Lately, I've had a bad habit of thinking too much, trying to analyze things that don't need analyzing.

Lewis is happier these days. We all are.

He showed off his high-def TV. Then he suggested we all go to the late show at the Fear Street Acres Cineplex. It seemed like a good idea.

I had no way of knowing that halfway through the movie, the horror would return for me.

4

It was a midnight show of an Adam
Sandler comedy. So dumb, we all started calling out our own jokes. We were just about the
only ones in the theater, so it really didn't
matter.

Shark was doing a very good imitation of
Adam Sandler. He even got up and did a
funny walk up and down the aisle. We were
hooting and laughing. And then someone sitting in the back complained. And a skinny
little guy in a red blazer, who looked about
twelve and had a high, cracking voice, came
and told us we'd have to leave if we didn't
chill.

So we quieted down, although we couldn't
stop giggling. And then Clark spilled all the
change from his pocket. It clattered over the

floor. And we started laughing and goofing all over again.

I slid down in my chair and raised my knees to the seat in front of me. Adam Sandler was chasing after Drew Barrymore, and I thought, whoa, he looks a lot like Lewis. Except Lewis is not so geeky-looking.

Shark was still imitating Adam Sandler. Nikki shoved him, pleading with him to stop. Dana and Clark had their arms around each other and were lip-locked, totally ignoring the movie.

I suddenly felt drowsy. It had been a long day. I had a very long Chem test in the morning. After school, I had to take care of my little brother Danny and make him dinner. Taking care of Danny can make *anyone* tired. He's like a tornado or something. He actually bounces off the walls!

So I started feeling tired. I guess my eyes closed. I wasn't really following the film. Maybe I dozed off for a few minutes. I'm not sure.

When I opened my eyes, it took a while for the screen to come into focus. Drew Barrymore had been a blonde in this movie.

Why did she suddenly have dark hair?

I gasped when I recognized the face. Not Drew Barrymore's face. *My* face.

Yes, I saw myself on the screen.

Blinking hard, I lowered my legs and pulled myself up straight. I felt a cold tingle at the back of my neck. Squinting hard, I watched Lewis walk onto the movie screen. He was wearing Adam Sandler's jeans and red-checked shirt. But it was definitely Lewis, and he had a very frightened expression on his face.

I raised my hands to my cheeks and stared as another figure walked into the scene. A woman. I didn't recognize her at first.

On the screen, my expression changed. My eyes bulged in fear. I watched Lewis grab my hand. The woman turned. *Angelica Fear!* I recognized her cold, clear eyes, her high cheekbones, the cruel, thin-lipped smile on her pretty face.

She appeared solid at first, but then she faded until I could see through her. Transparent now, like a movie ghost.

On-screen, she floated over me. My hands flew up to protect myself. I watched myself stumble back against the wall. Where were we? A house I didn't recognize.

Staring in horror at the movie screen, I knew what Angelica was doing. She was trying to possess me again. She floated over me, then started to lower herself.

In the movie scene, Lewis uttered a cry. He grabbed for her waist with both hands to try to pull her away from me. But his hands shot through her transparent body. He grabbed only air.

On-screen, I tried to run, but she held me in place. I saw her dropping into me, her legs disappearing first. Sliding . . . sliding down until her waist poked down into my head and we appeared like some kind of terrifying con-joined twins.

Angelica was possessing me again, and I couldn't escape.

I watched Lewis leaping high, grabbing at her. Grabbing at nothing as she slid lower, lower into my body.

As I stared at the screen, I gripped the chair in front of me, gripped it tightly until my hands ached.

And I watched Angelica Fear disappear inside my body. I watched the terrifying scene on the huge screen in front of me, and my whole body shook as if jolted in an earthquake.

Without even realizing it, I stood up—and opened my mouth in an ear-shattering scream of horror.

5

Lewis pulled me out to the lobby. The skinny guy in the red blazer had a broom and dustpan in his hands. He stared at me blankly.

"I . . . saw us," I told Lewis, my whole body trembling. "I saw us—on the screen."

He put his arm around me and guided me out the glass doors.

"Anything wrong?" I heard the red-blazer guy call before the door swung shut.

My friends came bursting out after us. Shark carried his huge bucket of popcorn. Dana grabbed my hand. "Jamie, you're shaking. What *happened*?"

"I . . . I'm not crazy," I stammered. "But I saw Lewis and me on the screen. Angelica Fear, too."

I stopped there. Shark, Nikki, and Clark

didn't know anything about Angelica Fear possessing me, forcing me to do those murders. And I didn't want them to know.

Dana squeezed my hand between both of hers. "Jamie, your eyes were closed," she said. "I saw you sleeping. Really. It was a dream."

I shook my head. "No. I was awake. I know I was."

Lewis had his arm around me. The others stared at me as if I were crazy.

Shark stuffed a handful of popcorn into his mouth. "You freaked us all out," he said, chewing. "It *had* to be a nightmare. I didn't see you up on the screen!"

"I've been having nightmares too," Nikki muttered.

"Sometimes they're, like, totally real," Clark said. "Because you remember them more than *good* dreams. One night I had this nightmare I couldn't jump off the floor to make a layup. My shoes were suddenly too heavy and—"

"I . . . just want to go home," I said, unable to shake off the feeling of terror. "Sorry I ruined the movie for everyone."

"You didn't ruin it. Adam Sandler ruined it!" Shark joked. I knew he was trying to snap me out of it, but it wasn't working.

Lewis offered to drive me home. But I didn't want to explain any more to him, either. I kissed him on the cheek. Then I said good night to everyone, apologized again, and hurried off with Dana to my dad's car.

We drove home in silence. I stared out at the dark houses and empty yards.

It was late. After midnight. My parents had gone to bed. Dana followed me into my room. Sighing, I pulled off my sneakers and dropped onto my bed.

Dana slid the desk chair over and sat down. Her normally pale cheeks were flushed from the cold. Her eyes kept studying me. "Feeling better?"

I shrugged. "I feel like such a jerk," I said. "Everyone was having a good time. Lewis is in such a good mood. And what do I do? I bring everyone down."

Dana smoothed a strand of wavy black hair off her forehead. "They don't know what you've been through," she said softly.

"Do you really think it was a dream?" I asked. "I thought I was awake. It seemed so real. It made sense. It didn't jump all over the place like a dream."

"I saw your eyes close," she replied. She frowned at me. "Listen, Jamie, I know what happened to you. I was there. I saw how totally horrifying it was. I still dream about it too, you know?"

"I didn't know that," I said. "I guess—"

"But you've got to put it behind you," Dana said. "We all have to put the bad things behind us. I mean, everything is cool now. Jamie, you should be able to relax. You're totally back to normal. Look at you—you're not even limping anymore!"

She was right. Suddenly, about a month ago, I woke up and discovered my hip didn't hurt anymore. I could walk normally.

"A miracle recovery"—that's what my mom called it.

I wasn't sure *how* it had happened. I didn't want to think about it.

"Ever since we killed off Angelica Fear, things have been going great for everybody,"

Dana said. "I can't *believe* I won the Collings-worth Prize! Now I can afford college. I'm so happy."

She stood up and pumped her fist in the air. "I'm so happy," she repeated. "I never wanted anything so much in my life." Her cheeks were still red. Her dark eyes flashed with excitement.

Dana turned back to me. "Things are going well for you, too. You should be able to relax now, Jamie."

"I know," I said, biting my bottom lip. "But I can't. I know it's been four months since you destroyed Angelica. Four months that I've been free of her. But . . ."

My words caught in my throat. I took a deep breath. "But I keep thinking she's still around," I choked out. "I just have this feeling. That she's coming back . . . to possess me again. I . . . I can't stop thinking about it."

Dana sighed. The light faded in her eyes. "You've got to," she said softly. "You've got to put it behind you, Jamie. This is your senior year of high school. You want to enjoy the rest of it, don't you?"

I nodded. "Of course. But—"

"So you've got to tell yourself it's over and done. She went up in a fume of green gas. She's gone, Jamie. And she isn't coming back."

I opened my mouth to reply, but I didn't get the words out.

The window rattled.

I saw a hand reach in from outside.

A dark figure pushing against the glass.

"It's her!" I screamed. "It's Angelica Fear!"

6

Dana grabbed me by the shoulders and held me. We both stood beside the bed and watched as Lewis lowered himself into the room.

I gasped.

Why had I pictured Angelica Fear again?

Lewis tossed his parka on the bed and hurried over to me. "Jamie—are you okay? You used to love it when I climbed the gutter up to your room."

"I . . . I'm sorry," I murmured. I hugged him and held on to him.

"She's totally obsessed," Dana said. She had her arms crossed defensively. She started to pace back and forth. "She keeps seeing Angelica Fear everywhere."

Lewis kept his eyes on mine. "I don't

look anything like Angelica Fear," he said.

I knew he was making a joke. I forced a laugh. "I can't help it," I said. "I just have a feeling she isn't gone. That she's still nearby."

Lewis grinned. "Did you look under the bed?"

I rolled my eyes. "Ha-ha."

"When I was little, I was terrified to go to bed at night," Lewis said, dropping into my desk chair. "My mom read me a picture book called *The Monster Who Lived Under the Bed*. And I believed it. I believed there was a fat, ugly monster hiding under my bed. I used to scream and cry when my parents took me up to my room every night."

"So what happened?" I asked. "How did you get over it?"

"I didn't," he said. "I still scream and cry every night."

I groaned. "Give me a break, Lewis."

Dana laughed. "I believe it." She gave him a playful shove that almost knocked him off the chair.

I shivered. "I believe in monsters now," I said. "Real monsters. Maybe I'll worry about

Angelica Fear for the rest of my life."

Lewis wasn't watching me. He had his eyes lowered to the bottom shelf of my bookcase. "What's that?" he asked, pointing.

I crossed the room to see what he was staring at. "It's an old spellbook," I told him. "You know. The one I took from that secret room in the Fear Mansion."

Dana reached down and lifted the old book from the bottom shelf. "Whoa. It weighs a ton."

"I have an idea," Lewis said. A grin spread slowly over his face. "They don't call me 'The Brain' for nothing."

"They *don't* call you 'The Brain,'" Dana said. "I've never heard anyone call you 'The Brain.'"

"Shut up," Lewis said. "Put the spellbook down on the desk. I'm going to prove that Angelica Fear is gone."

My mouth dropped open. "How are you going to do that? Cast a spell?"

He shook his head. "No. *You* are."

Dana let out an impatient sigh. "Lewis, do you have to be so mysterious? Tell us what brilliant plan you're cooking up."

He raised both hands, as if in surrender. "Okay, okay." His expression turned serious. "Jamie, when you were possessed by Angelica, you cast spells from this book—right?"

I nodded. "Yeah. I cast spells on Dana to make her go faint and pass out."

Dana rolled her eyes. "Good times."

"Well, go ahead," Lewis said, waving me toward the book. "Try to cast that same spell on Dana right now."

"Whoa! Wait a minute!" Dana cried. "This is your great idea? It sucks!"

"Listen to me," Lewis insisted. "The spell will fail, don't you see? Because Angelica is gone. She isn't here. Jamie, the only reason you could do those spells was because you were possessed by Angelica and you had her evil amulet."

"Okay . . . ," I said. "So?"

"So she's gone. Go ahead. Try the spell. It will fail because she's gone for good."

I turned to Dana. "Are you okay with this?"

She shrugged. "If it will convince you."

I hesitated. "Too dangerous," I murmured. "If it works—"

"It can't work!" Lewis insisted. "Dana killed Angelica, remember? *No way* your spell will work."

Dana walked up to the desk and opened the book. "Come on. Let's get it over with so I can go to bed."

"I can't," I said, shaking my head. "I can't do that to Dana again. Really—"

"Okay. Do it to me," Lewis said, taking my hand. He pulled me in front of the open spellbook. "Find the spell, Jamie. And do it on me. I'm not scared because I know it won't work. You'll see."

Dana and Lewis stood at my sides, staring at me, urging me to do this dangerous thing. Was it a good test? I wondered. Would it help me finally relax?

Maybe.

"Okay," I said. I began turning the crinkly, yellowed pages of the old book, searching for the spell. "Here it is."

I ran my finger down the page, squinting at

the tiny type. "Yes. I have a dim memory of it. This is the spell I used on Dana."

"Go ahead. Blast away. Let me have it!" Lewis said cheerfully. Much too cheerfully.

He really was convinced I could no longer do spells.

I hoped he was right.

Dana and I pulled the black candles from the back of the closet, where I had hidden them away. We placed them in a circle and lit them one by one.

I lowered myself to my knees inside the circle of flickering candles. Dana handed me the spellbook. Cradling it in my arms, I slowly, almost silently, began to chant the ancient words.

They were nonsense syllables to me. I whispered the words, sounding them out as I read.

The room hushed as I read—so quiet, I could hear the tick of the grandfather clock outside my room at the end of the hall.

After a few minutes of reading the ancient words, I neared the end of the spell. Squinting in the candlelight, I raised my eyes to Lewis.

And let out a cry.

His eyes . . . They were closed. His head had rolled back on his shoulders. His mouth hung open.

In a trance. Out cold.

7

"Lewis?"

My heart skipped a beat. I grabbed him by the shoulders and started to shake him.

He opened his eyes. A smile spread over his face. "Gotcha," he said. "Just kidding."

"Ooh, you jerk!" I tried to slug him, but he wrapped his arms around me and hugged me. "How could you *do* that?"

"See?" he said, still holding on to me so I couldn't hit him. "Your spells don't work anymore, Jamie. So lighten up."

I pushed him away gently. "I . . . I guess you're right," I said.

Dana bent to blow out the candles. "Lewis is definitely right," she said. "So try to put it in the past. We have to try to make the rest of senior year really *rock*. It's the last senior year we'll ever have."

I laughed. "I hope so. Lewis and I had our senior year *last* year. We never planned on doing it all over again."

"Just forget about that," Dana scolded. She yawned. "Hey, maybe your spell *did* work. I'm totally wiped."

I looked at her. All the color had drained from her face. She became totally pale whenever she got tired. "Go get some sleep," I said. "Sorry I was such a downer tonight."

"That's okay," she replied. "You're a downer *every* night." We laughed. She gave Lewis and me a wave and headed up to her room in the attic.

As soon as she was gone, Lewis grabbed me, pulled me to him, and kissed me. We stood like that, holding the kiss for a long time.

I was breathing hard when he finally pulled away. "Everything's going to be great now," he whispered.

I smiled back at him. "I hope so."

I pulled his face to mine. I kissed him

again. Then I pressed my face against his cheek and held on to him.

Gazing over his shoulder, my eyes stopped at the open spellbook on the floor. I squinted down at it.

Something moved across the pages.

It took me a long while to realize what I was seeing.

The letters . . . they were moving.

The letters on the page were sliding around, rearranging themselves.

I stared in disbelief. Stared over Lewis's shoulder, watching the letters skip and slide, moving up and down and around the pages . . . until finally they stopped.

And I gaped in frozen horror at the words they had spelled out:

THE EVIL LIVES.

PART TWO

PART TWO

8

Friday after school, I stood at my locker, shuffling through my backpack. My water bottle had spilled, and half of my binders were soaked. Groaning, I pulled the half-empty bottle out and rummaged at the bottom of the pack for the missing cap.

Glancing up, I saw Dana across the hall. She was talking to Nate Garvin. She had her hands at her waist and a scowl on her face. Reading her body language, I could see she definitely wasn't enjoying the conversation.

Dana and Nate had been hooking up for a while. Until Nate started to believe that Dana was responsible for the murders of the two girls in our class.

That really hurt Dana. She felt totally betrayed by Nate. "He should have believed in me," she said. "I trusted him, and he turned on me just like that."

That was last November. Now it was March. I knew she hadn't spoken to him since then.

Now I watched Nate turn away from her and walk off down the emptying hall. Dana came trotting over to me, still scowling.

"What's up with Nate?" I asked.

She let out a growl, clasping her hands into tight fists. "He keeps pestering me. Says we should go out. He wants to get back together."

I found the water bottle lid at the bottom of the backpack. I pulled it out and screwed it back onto the bottle. "And?"

"And what?" Dana snapped. "No way. No way I'd ever go out with Nate again. Did he stand up for me when everyone thought I was a murderer? No, he didn't."

Her dark eyes glowed with anger. She clasped and unclasped her fists. Finally, she took a deep breath and started to calm down.

"Who needs Nate?" she said. "I'm really into Clark." She smiled. "I've never gone out with a sports star before. He's such a good guy. And on TV last night, they said he's the best point guard the Tigers have ever had."

"Cool," I murmured. I started tugging out the wet binders and wiping them off with my wool scarf.

"Are you and Lewis coming to the bonfire next week?" Dana asked. "You know. To cheer the team on and all that school spirit stuff?"

"Yeah, we're coming," I said. "I've never seen a mile-high bonfire."

"I don't think it's really that high," Dana said. "But it's going to be fun. I just think it's totally cool that Shadyside is going to the state tournament. First time in ten years! I'm excited, and I've only been here a few months!"

"Rah-rah," I said, mopping up my Psych textbook.

She finally noticed what I was doing. "Jamie, your stuff is all wet."

"Duh," I said. "Don't you enjoy dumping a bottle of water on all your books?"

"Can I help?"

I shook my head. "Do you ever think about the amulet?" I asked. The words jumped out. I don't know where the thought came from.

She narrowed her eyes at me. "The amulet? Well, yes. Sometimes. Why?"

"Because it's out there somewhere," I said. I let the backpack fall to the floor. "And don't tell me to calm down and put it in the past and forget about it."

She gasped. I guess my strong emotion shocked her.

"A bird flew into my garage," I continued. I'd started this—now I couldn't stop. "A one-eyed blackbird, right?"

She nodded and glanced around the hallway to make sure no one could hear.

"It swooped in while Angelica Fear was dying inside the burning kiln. It picked up her amulet and flew out the garage window with it."

"Yes, yes, yes," Dana cried. "We've been over this a hundred times. Why are you bringing it up again, Jamie?"

"Because the amulet is still out there," I said. "Wouldn't you feel better if you knew where it was?"

She sighed. "That bird probably used it to build a nest."

"How do we know that?" I asked. "Dana, how do we know?"

My friends and I have a secret life.

We call ourselves the Night People. We sneak out of our houses after midnight, after our parents are asleep. And we meet on Fear Street at a bar called Nights.

Some nights we hang out at the bar until three or four in the morning. Other nights we go around town, just goofing and having our own private time. The world is ours then. The whole town is asleep. Houses dark. Cars parked for the night.

Lewis and I were the first Night People. It was senior year, and we were too busy to see each other. So we started meeting after midnight.

Soon, word got out and other kids started joining us. Shark and Nate were regulars, and Shark's cute girlfriend, Nikki, from Waynesbridge High in the next town. Aaron and Galen showed up just about every night, and some other kids.

It was our biggest secret. Our private night world. We loved it. Sometimes I thought about it all day.

Friday night, I fell asleep and didn't wake up till nearly two. I sneaked out of the house and hurried to Fear Street.

Stepping into the bar, I greeted Ryland O'Connor, the bartender, and waved to my friends. Nights was built on the spot where the Fear Mansion had stood. There's a brass plaque on the wall when you walk in. It shows Simon and Angelica Fear.

We all kiss the plaque when we come into the bar. Partly as a joke and partly for good luck.

I gave the plaque a quick peck and hurried to join Dana and Lewis at a table near the front. As I sat down, I saw Shark, Nate, and Nikki at their usual booth against the back wall. Aaron and Galen were in the next booth, arm wrestling. They had a red-haired girl with them I didn't recognize.

"Where were you?" Lewis asked. He signaled Ryland to bring two beers.

"Sleeping," I said.

He squinted at me. "Sleeping? Who has time for sleeping?"

The front door swung open, and Clark walked in, wearing his maroon and gray Shadyside letter jacket.

"Go, Tigers!"

"Tigers rock!"

The bar erupted in applause and shouts. Clark waved both fists in the air and shouted along with them.

"I didn't know we were at a pep rally," Lewis said, laughing.

Shark came shambling over to our table. I could tell he'd had more than a few beers. He wore a gray hoodie with the hood up, and vintage jeans.

He raised his beer bottle in a toast to Clark. "Tigers KILL!" he shouted. He and Clark bumped knuckles and slapped high fives.

We drank a lot of beers. We were all in a good mood. By two A.M., I think we were pretty trashed.

"Yo, dude—let's go out and have some fun tonight!" Shark cried. His eyes were wild. He kind of slurred.

Lewis jumped up. "Yeah, let's rock!" he shouted. "The town belongs to us!"

Kids jumped up to follow Shark and Lewis out the door. Dana and I exchanged glances. "Lewis has changed," Dana murmured. "Did he used to be so *bold*?"

I watched him slapping Shark on the back. "I think he's finally feeling better," I told her. "I think the accident is finally behind him."

I noticed Nate had his eyes on Dana. He started over to her, but she quickly pushed back her chair and ran after Clark.

Carrying beer bottles, a bunch of us started half-trotting, half-walking down Fear Street, traveling in a pack. Clark began singing the Tigers' fight song, and everyone joined in.

It was a cold, clear night. We could see our breath puff up in front of us as we sang. A million stars gleamed in the blue-black night sky.

"The Night People rule!" Shark shouted up at the sky.

Nate grabbed his shoulder. "Cool it, dude. We don't want to wake anyone."

Shark giggled and tilted his beer bottle to his mouth. He finished it and heaved the bottle down the street. It landed with a crash of shattering glass.

Clark grabbed Shark's arm and spun him around. "Come on, man. We don't want anyone to know we're out here."

He was right. We'd been able to keep the Night People a secret for nearly two years because we were careful not to cause any real trouble.

"Shark, how many beers did you have?" Nate asked.

Shark held up three fingers. "Five," he said, and started giggling again.

Nate held up four fingers and stared at them. "You mean five," he said, waving his hand in Shark's face.

They both fell to their knees in the middle of the street. Clark and Nikki struggled to pull them up.

We walked past dark houses and empty driveways. Dana and I walked side by side behind Aaron and Galen. I'd forgotten my gloves, so I kept my hands in my parka pockets.

A big, furry dog came loping at us from

the side of a house. His tail wagged hard. He circled us three or four times. I think he was lonely and was happy to have some company.

Galen stooped down to pet him. Galen loves dogs. He told me he plans to be a vet after college. His parents won't let him have a dog because they have asthma and they say they're allergic.

After a few minutes, the dog took off, running down the middle of the street. We all ran after him, weaving and stumbling, calling out different dog names, trying to see if we could make him turn around.

We were all completely totaled. We didn't know *what* we were doing.

"Whoa. Check it out!"

Shark's cry made us all stop. Shark pointed to a tall, brick house half-hidden by a row of fat evergreen trees. Squinting into the shadows, I saw three kids' bikes leaning against the side of the house.

Shark giggled. "How about a r-r-race?" he slurred. He took off, running across the grass. Lewis, Galen, Nate, Clark, and some others followed him up to the house.

Dana and I watched from the sidewalk. "This is not a good idea," Dana murmured. "I'm totally drunk, and I still know it's a bad idea."

"They're just having some fun," I said.

Shark, Galen, and Lewis came down to the street, walking the kids' bikes at their sides. "This is a race to the dead end at Walker Street," Shark said. He climbed onto his bike and squeezed the hand brakes several times. Perching on that little bike, he looked totally stupid.

He grinned at Galen and Lewis. "Loser buys beers for everyone."

"Hey, I'm outta this," Galen said, shaking his head. "I'm broke. And . . . and I feel a little sick." He hurried to the curb. He bent over and tried to throw up.

Clark grabbed the handlebars. "I'll do it. If you guys want to concede now, I'll understand."

Lots of laughter.

Shark gave Clark a friendly shove. "I'm going to kick your ass."

"Don't touch him. He's a star!" Aaron shouted.

More laughter.

I glanced to the house. I hoped all the loud voices wouldn't wake up the owners of the bikes.

"Just have your race before we all freeze!" I exclaimed.

Lewis leaned forward on his little bike. "Dudes, let's make it a little harder," he said. "How about 'No Hands'?"

Everyone cheered. Shark shrugged. "Why not? You two are *still* losers."

Dana grabbed my parka sleeve. "Come on. Let's go to the finish line."

We started to jog to the dead end, three blocks away. Nate and Nikki and some of the others followed us. "Is this crazy or what?" Nikki asked me in her breathy, little-girl voice.

"We used to have fun like this all the time," I said.

She squinted at me. "Shut *up*! Fun? We're *freezing* out here! And *they're* racing on stolen kids' bikes. What are they *thinking*? Let's say a cop car comes by—"

"Let's *not* say it!" I replied. "Check it out.

The race has started. Hey—Clark is killing them already!"

We turned and gazed into the circles of light from the streetlamps. And watched the three bikes rolling toward us. All three guys were pedaling ferociously, their hands high in the air.

The bikes were weaving wildly from curb to curb. I think all three guys were too drunk to realize it. They couldn't pedal a straight line if they tried!

"They're *flying!*" Nate shouted.

"Go, Clark! Go, Clark!" Dana started to chant.

As the bikes rolled toward us down a steep hill, we all forgot about how late it was and we started shouting and cheering. And then the cheers stopped as we saw Clark's bike shoot out of control.

Dana screamed. I grabbed her arm.

Clark came zigzagging down the street so fast, and the little bike swerved away from the other two racers. His hands were still above his head as it slammed into the back of an SUV parked at the curb.

I heard a loud *crunnnch* that sounded like

metal ripping apart. And then we all cried out as Clark went flying.

He sailed off the bike, did a wild flip in the air, and landed hard on his back on the SUV roof.

The bike bounced off the bumper of the big car, rolled to the curb, and toppled onto its side, tires spinning.

Clark didn't move.

Hands pressed to the sides of my face, I stared at his body on the car roof, arms outstretched, legs sprawled over the sides.

No one uttered a sound. We all went running to the SUV.

I got there first. I grabbed his hand. His arm fell limply toward me. He still didn't move.

"He's dead!" I screamed, my voice breaking. "Another kid in our class! It's happened again!"

9

I held on to his limp, lifeless hand.

Dana pushed me aside. "It can't be!" she cried. "It *can't* be!"

I heard the other two bikes clatter to the pavement. Shark fell onto his stomach on the pavement. Lewis came running over.

"Is he okay? Should we call 911?" Lewis called breathlessly.

"I . . . I'm okay," Clark murmured. He slowly raised his head.

I gasped. "Clark—?"

He pulled himself up on one elbow and shook his head, trying to clear it. "I think I'm okay." He tested his arms and hands. "Just had my breath knocked out."

I let out a long, relieved sigh. Dana and I helped pull him down off the SUV roof.

His knees buckled. We had to hold him up.

But after a few seconds, he shook us away and turned to Shark and Lewis. "Hey, who won the race?"

Shark looked up from the pavement. "You lost," he said.

"Clark buys for everyone!" Nate chimed in.

"Shut up! I don't think that's fair," Nikki said, pushing back her streaked blond hair and snuggling up against Shark.

"Hey, guys, we'd better return the bikes," Aaron said. He picked up Clark's bike from the gutter. "Oh, wow. Totally mangled. Way to go, Clark."

The front wheel was bent like a pretzel.

Aaron, Shark, and Nate walked the three little bikes back to the house. "Whose idea was 'No Hands'?" Clark asked.

Lewis put his arm around my shoulders as we walked. "Jamie, you all right?" he said softly. "Did you really think Clark was dead?"

I sucked in a deep breath of cold air. "He . . . he didn't move," I said. "And . . . I guess I'm just frightened. I always think something horrible is going to happen."

Lewis stopped and pulled me into his arms. He hugged me and pressed his warm face against my cold cheek. "It's okay," he whispered. "See? Clark is perfectly fine."

"I know," I said, pressing my forehead against his. "My mind . . . it just automatically—"

I stopped. And turned to the house. The front lights flashed on!

The three guys were still parking the bikes against the wall. "RUN!" Clark screamed, waving frantically for them to *move*. "RUN!"

Shark, Aaron, and Clark took off, their shoes slipping in the dew-wet grass. We all ran, heading off in different directions.

Lewis and I moved side by side toward the bar on Fear Street. I didn't turn back until I was at the end of the next block. Gasping for breath, I stared down the street.

No one was coming after us. Maybe we all got away.

Lewis and I jogged the rest of the way, moving slower now, relaxing the pace, my heartbeats slowing to normal. The cold air felt refreshing on my hot face.

"My car's right there," Lewis said, pointing. "Want a ride home?"

I hesitated. "No. I think I want to keep jogging. It feels really good. I need to run off some of my anxiety, I guess. And now that my leg and hip are healed, it feels so great to run."

He kissed me good night. I watched him climb into his car and drive away. Then I turned and started jogging down the middle of the street.

I made my way past the Fear Street Acres shopping center. A few stores had their window displays lit, but the parking lot was empty. In the daytime, this street would be jammed with cars. But now it was all mine.

My shoes thudded the pavement in a steady, slow rhythm. All mine. The street was mine alone. Soon, the lights of the shopping center were behind me, and I moved into a deep darkness as the street curved through what was left of the Fear Street Woods.

Gnarly old trees leaned over the street, their bare branches shivering over my head. I picked up my pace a little. Only a few blocks from my house now.

I could hear my steady foot beats and the rush of wind through the old trees. Very soothing, I thought. Totally relaxing.

And then I listened hard as I heard another sound. A sound that didn't belong.

A fluttering. Soft at first and then louder ... until it sounded like the flap of a paper kite in the wind.

Glancing up, I saw the large bird flying low over my head. A blackbird.

I stopped running, my heart pounding now.

It *can't* be the same blackbird! I told myself.

It swooped over my head, turned, and flew back, hovering low.

It *can't* be the same bird.

But then it raised itself and spread its wings. It turned, and I saw its head clearly. And I saw the missing eye.

A one-eyed blackbird!

"No!" The cry escaped my lips, and I started to run again.

The wings beat loudly over my head. The bird followed me down the street, ducking under the tree limbs, swooping past me, then darting back.

It had its talons raised high in front of it. Lifting its wings, it floated low, its single eye glowing with excitement.

I couldn't run any farther. I turned and faced it. And shook my fist in the air. "Go away!" I screamed. "Leave me ALONE!"

10

I guess Jamie isn't a bird lover.

She certainly didn't seem glad to see me.

Why did I do that? I guess for the fun of it. I wasn't really torturing her. You can't accuse me of that.

I'm not quite ready to torture her. But I shall be soon.

I like to keep her tense and worried. I want them all to worry.

After all, they have a lot to worry about.

They can have their late-night fun, sneaking out after midnight and going off on their harmless adventures. I enjoy it too. I'm right there with them, after all.

I'm always with them.

And you sense it—don't you, Jamie?

You sense that I'm always there with you, always watching and waiting.

Well, you won't have to wait long.

I can't allow the fun to continue much longer. Not with the anger that burns in my heart. Not with the rage that drives me to revenge.

You have a lot more to fear than a swooping blackbird, Jamie, dear.

A lot more to FEAR.

11

Saturday afternoon, I was in my room when Dana walked in. She had her hair tied back in a ponytail, and she wore loose-fitting gray sweats with stains on the front of the shirt.

"You look about ten with your hair pulled back like that," I said. "What have you been doing?"

"Helping your mom make soup," she said, brushing off the sweatshirt. "Look. Carrot hands. I've been peeling carrots for an hour."

"So many?"

She laughed. "Your brother kept eating them as fast as I peeled them. He's like a rabbit!" Her smile faded. She stared at the book in my lap. "What's that?"

"The spellbook," I said. "It doesn't have an index or anything. It's impossible to find what you're looking for."

She dropped down beside me on the bed. "What are you looking for?"

"Something about blackbirds," I said, gazing down at the pages of tiny type. "A spell, maybe, to get rid of them."

Dana sighed and rolled her eyes.

"That blackbird took the amulet," I said. "And now it's following me. Watching me. That's not normal—right? Stop looking at me like that, Dana."

She grabbed my arm. "Jamie, you've got to stop obsessing about this. You've been in your room all day reading this book. You've got to get out of the house and stop thinking about birds and amulets and magic."

She jumped up. "Come on. Let's go out. There's a big flea market in the parking lot at school. Let me get changed, and then we'll go check it out. Maybe we'll find some cool vintage stuff."

I folded down a page to mark my place. My mind was still on the book. "I memorized a spell," I told her. "I think I could use it to summon Angelica Fear."

Dana groaned.

"No. Really," I insisted. "I think—"

"Are you crazy?" Dana cried. "Why on earth would you want to call her back?"

"To confront her," I said. "To find out the truth. So I could know for sure about the amulet. And to make sure she isn't coming back to possess me again."

Dana shook her head. "I can't take this anymore. Jamie, why don't you worry about college rejections instead? Or worry about world hunger or something?"

She closed the spellbook, slid it off my lap, and pulled me to my feet. "Come on. We're going to the flea market. We're going to look at old clothes and stuff. We're going to gossip about kids at school. And we're not going to think about anything serious."

I laughed. "Sounds like a plan."

It was a windy, gray afternoon, but the flea market was jammed with people. I saw a few kids from school, and I recognized a lot of parents.

The big canvas banner announcing the flea market was flapping in the gusts of wind and seemed about to fly off the fence. A rack of vintage jeans had blown over, and two people were struggling to stand it up again.

One side of the parking lot was lined with food stalls. I saw a cotton candy booth and a booth selling Sno-Kones and ice cream. We started past a booth where they were grilling up hot dogs and sausages. I took a deep breath, inhaling the tangy aroma, and realized I hadn't eaten all day.

So Dana and I stopped for a hot dog and a Diet Coke. We watched a large woman in a ratty fur coat leaning over a table, pawing furiously through a pile of wool sweaters. Two little kids ran by, chasing each other. The little girl had a red helium balloon floating on a string, and the boy kept trying to pull it down.

I swallowed the last of the hot dog. I'd downed it in about five seconds, and I immediately wanted three more. But I've got to watch my perfect figure, right?

Dana and I waved to two cheerleaders we knew. They were helping out at a thrift shop charity table. We started wandering through the aisles, checking out the stuff.

Dana held up a sheet of fake tattoos. Mostly snakes and red and blue flowers and stars. "Do I need this?"

"No," I said.

But she bought it, anyway, and stuffed it into her bag. "You can never have enough tattoos," she said, pulling me to the next table.

We talked about Marci Hyland at school, who got a *real* tattoo on her back just above her butt. Chinese letters in black. She says she doesn't know what they say. She was totally trashed when she got it.

Now she's afraid to wear low-riding jeans around the house. Because she hasn't had the nerve to tell her parents about the tattoo.

I stopped at the next table and bought some white athletic socks. Four pairs for five dollars. Exciting, right?

We ran into some of Clark's friends from the basketball team. They were on their way to a practice in the gym. We talked about the bonfire pep rally next weekend. They said they were tense, tired of waiting for the game with

Riverside. They wished the tournament started today.

They teased Dana about ruining Clark's concentration, taking his mind off the game.

"You're kidding, right?" Dana shot back. "*Nothing* can take his mind off the game. Believe me, I've tried!"

Big laughs.

The guys jogged off to the gym. Dana and I moved down the row of tables. The wind picked up, and I felt a few cold raindrops on my forehead.

"Hey, maybe we should get out of here," I said, glancing up at the darkening sky.

Some of the booth people started to cover their tables with plastic. A mother ran down the aisle, frantically calling her kids.

"Let's just check out this jewelry," Dana said, tugging me over to some glass display cases.

I bent down and squinted at the jeweled brooches and necklaces in one case. "It's all old," I said. "How do you feel about emeralds?"

Dana laughed. "I'm *for* them."

I moved to the next case. Silver and gold

bracelets lined up neatly in two rows. "Nice," I murmured.

Then I stopped—and stared.

My breath caught in my throat. I leaned closer to the glass.

"Oh, wow. I don't *believe* it!" I cried.

12

Dana pushed up beside me. "Jamie, what's wrong?"

I pointed to a bracelet near the bottom of the display case. "Look. It's . . . it's . . ." My heart pounded so hard, I could barely talk.

I waved to the young woman down at the end of the long table. She was talking to the woman behind the socks table. "Hi. Can I see a bracelet?"

She came walking over slowly. She wore a fleece jacket over a long black skirt. She had a Red Sox cap pulled backward over long, straight coppery hair that tumbled down her back. "My name is Melissa. Did you want to see something?" She pulled out a ring of keys from her jacket pocket.

"That silver bracelet," I said. "The one with the tiny blue jewels."

"That's a nice one," she said. She opened the display case, reached down the row of bracelets, and pulled it out. Then she rolled it around in her hand, examining it before she handed it to me.

I took it and held it up for Dana. "Don't you see? It's the same design as the amulet."

Dana squinted at it.

A strong gust of wind once again blew over the rack of vintage jeans at the end of the aisle. I felt more cold raindrops in the wind.

Dana nodded. "Yeah, it looks a lot like the amulet. The way the jewels are arranged in the silver."

I stared at it a while longer. I felt a tingling at the back of my neck. I turned to Melissa. "Can you tell me anything about this bracelet?"

She took it from me and studied it. "Well . . . I can tell you that it's very old."

"How old?" I asked. "A hundred years?"

She frowned. "Maybe. I couldn't really say. It belonged to my great-great-grandmother. I found it in a chest in her house after she died."

"Your great-great-grandmother? Was she a Fear?" I blurted out.

"Oh, heavens no!" she replied. The wind blew her cap off, and her long hair swirled around her face.

She brushed it back and bent to retrieve her cap.

"I'm sorry," I said. "I didn't mean—"

She smiled at me. She had a pretty smile. I noticed her hazel eyes, shaped like cat eyes, and her creamy, pale skin.

"She *worked* for the Fear family," she said, twisting the cap over her hair. "What made you mention the Fears?"

"Uh . . . I don't know," I replied. I didn't want to get into a whole thing about the amulet.

"Well, my great-great-grandmother was a housekeeper in the Fear Mansion for many years," Melissa continued. "I never thought about it. But maybe someone in the Fear family gave her this bracelet. You know. As a present."

She frowned again. "Although I've heard they weren't very generous people."

She handed the silver bracelet back to me. "Do you like it? Are you interested in buying it?"

The wind toppled a trash basket. Paper and other garbage blew down the aisle. The rain started to patter down harder.

I studied the bracelet. Yes, maybe it once belonged to the Fear family. Maybe it had magical powers . . . like the amulet.

"How much do you want for it?" Dana asked Melissa.

"It's a hundred dollars," she replied. "I'll take off the tax and make it a hundred even."

She turned the baseball cap around to keep the rain off her face. A streak of lightning brightened the sky. "I'd better start closing up," she said. She hurried to the other end of the table and started carrying display cases to a nearby cart.

"I don't have a hundred dollars," I told Dana. I searched my wallet. "I only have thirty."

"I only have change," Dana said. "I guess we can't buy it."

"Hey—!" Someone grabbed me from behind.

I spun around and found Lewis grinning at me. "Whassup, babe?"

I showed him the bracelet. "I really want this," I said. "But I can't afford it. It's a hundred bucks. You have any money?"

He snickered. "Money? What's money?"

I twirled the bracelet between my fingers. "I really need this."

Lewis looked down the table. "Where's the seller? Maybe we can make a deal? You know. Bargain."

Melissa had disappeared. "She's loading up her stuff," I said. "They're closing the flea market." I set the bracelet down on top of the display case. The blue jewels glowed, even in the dim, darkening light.

"Let's get out of here," Lewis said, taking my arm. "Come on, Dana. Want to cruise around? You know. See if anyone else is around?"

"Three's a crowd," Dana said, waving and starting to jog toward the school. "I'm going to go watch Clark practice for a while."

I watched her run off, ducking her head against the rain. Then I followed Lewis to his car, parked at the front of the school.

I dropped into the front seat, shivering. I swept back my rain-wet hair with both hands. Lewis lowered himself behind the wheel and grinned at me.

"Why are you grinning like that?" I asked.

He shrugged. "Just grinning." He started the car and pulled into the traffic of people leaving the flea market, fleeing the rain.

"What did you do today?" I asked.

"Helped my dad. He wanted to put in this electric garage door thing. You know. To make it go up and down. We spent hours on it, but we couldn't get it to work."

"So what happened?"

"He ran out of patience. He threw the controller on the concrete floor and stomped on it. Smashed it to bits." Lewis snickered. "You know my dad. He's about as patient as a pro wrestler."

I settled back on the seat. "Your dad does kinda look big and tough."

"He played hockey in college," Lewis said, turning onto Main Street. "He's always bragging about how he knocked a guy's teeth out."

"Awesome," I muttered.

"Hey, here," Lewis said. He pulled something from his jacket pocket and shoved it into my hand. "I got you a present."

"A present?" I stared at it.

The bracelet.

"Are you *kidding* me?" I screamed. "You *stole* it?"

He nodded, laughing. "I got a five-fingered discount."

"But—but—Lewis!" I sputtered, squeezing the bracelet in my hand. "You can't do that! That's awful! That woman was really nice."

"You said you wanted it," he replied, eyes straight ahead. For an instant, I glimpsed something different in his eyes, something flat and cold. Eyes I'd never seen before.

Rain pattered the windshield. We were driving through the Old Village, the oldest part of Shadyside.

"But that's not like you!" I cried. "Since when do you steal bracelets from people?"

"It's the *new* me," he said. He braked for a red light.

"But—but—"

"Hey, you said you really wanted it," he

said sharply. He took the bracelet from me and slipped it onto my wrist.

The silver felt cool against my skin. The blue jewels gleamed dully in the light from the streetlamp outside the car window.

I stared at Lewis. I didn't know what to say.

The light changed, and he stepped on the gas pedal. Soon, we were driving past farm country, empty fields, dark and bare. He clicked on the CD player. The new 50 Cent CD burst from the speakers. He cranked it up until the sound boomed off the windows.

"I love just cruising, going nowhere," he said.

I raised my arm and gazed at the bracelet. I brought it close to my face to study the jewels.

And as I did, I heard a voice, just a whisper—but loud enough to be heard over the booming music.

"I'm here, Jamie. I'm still here with you."

13

Well, that totally freaked me out. The whispered words haunted me. I couldn't get them out of my head.

I hid the bracelet in the back of my bottom dresser drawer. But that didn't help me get much sleep at night.

Why did I want that bracelet so badly? What did I think it would do for me?

I couldn't answer those questions, which made it all even scarier for me. I mean, what if it wasn't *me* who was so desperate to get her hands on the bracelet? What if it was Angelica Fear—*still inside me*—who made me desire it?

Thinking that made me sick. My stomach knotted up. I couldn't eat, and I had the *worst* stomachache.

I needed to confide in someone. But

Lewis was so cheerful and *up* these days, I didn't want to bring him down. And Dana was hardly around. She was totally involved with Clark, going to his practices and hanging out with the team. I think she was more excited about the state tournament than Clark was!

It was good to see Dana happy and excited too. I mean, she'd had such a horrible year with her mother dying, and her boyfriend back home drowning. And her father deciding he didn't want her and shipping her off to live with my family.

So, after all the horror we'd lived through, it was great to see Lewis and Dana getting it all together and enjoying the rest of senior year. I didn't want to spoil things for them.

But I just couldn't be happy like them. I couldn't forget the murders. And the evil woman who came back to life and possessed me and forced me to kill my friends.

How can you forget something like that?

And I couldn't lose the feeling that Angelica was still around. Still so close. Watching me. Waiting . . .

Tuesday night I couldn't sleep. So I got dressed and sneaked out of the house to join the Night People.

I walked into Nights, greeted by the familiar aroma of beer and cigarette smoke. I kissed the brass plaque on the wall, waved to Ryland O'Connor, and spotted Lewis sitting by himself in a booth against the back wall.

I saw Aaron and Galen with the red-haired girl I didn't know. The two guys were arm wrestling. The girl kept rolling her eyes. She looked totally embarrassed.

Then I saw Dana. She was in a booth at the side of the bar. I stopped. I couldn't help staring.

I blinked, thinking maybe I was hallucinating or something. But no. She was sitting on Nate's lap, kissing him, running her hands through his hair.

I turned away and strode the rest of the way to the back of the bar. "Did you see Dana with Nate?" I asked Lewis, sliding across from him.

He shrugged. "Weird, huh?" He was drinking a Diet Coke. He signaled Ryland to bring a beer for me. "How you doing, Jamie?"

"Not bad," I lied.

He looked down at my hands, clasped on the wooden tabletop. "Hey, where's the bracelet? You don't wear it?"

I shook my head. "I put it away," I told him. "It was kinda creepy. You know. Thinking maybe it was Angelica Fear's."

It was on the tip of my tongue to tell him about the whispers I'd heard. But I held myself back.

"I thought that's why you *wanted* the bracelet," he said.

I lowered my eyes. "I don't know *why* I wanted it. You really shouldn't have stolen it. Maybe that makes it *double* bad luck."

He laughed. "Jamie, have you been superstitious your whole life?"

I didn't answer. I heard familiar voices. Nikki and Shark. I didn't realize they were in the next booth.

Lewis said something else, but I didn't hear. I was eavesdropping on Nikki and Shark. Nikki sat right behind me. She was talking about Candy and Ada and Whitney. How they'd been murdered.

"It's so totally weird," Nikki was saying. "Those three girls who died. They were all Shadyside kids. No one at *my* school has died. Don't you see, Shark? It has to be some kind of bizarre curse on Shadyside High."

Shark said something, but I didn't hear it. I looked up to see Dana standing at the side of our booth.

She grabbed my hand and raised a finger to her lips with the other hand. "Not a word of this to Clark—okay?" she whispered.

I saw Nate standing at the front door to the bar, waiting for Dana. "But I thought you were serious about Clark," I said.

"I am," Dana replied. "But Nate is *so cute*! What can I do?" She spun away and trotted to the front to meet Nate. They disappeared out the door.

In the next booth, I heard Shark laugh. "Whoa. Nate's big night!"

"Didn't they break up?" Nikki asked.

Lewis grabbed my shoulder to get my attention. "Earth calling Jamie," he said. "Are you still here? I don't think you heard a word I said."

"Sorry," I murmured.

He was right. I hadn't been listening to him. I kept hearing Nikki's words repeating and repeating in my mind.

"A curse on Shadyside High . . ."

She couldn't be right—could she?

It didn't take long to find out. The next afternoon, the curse struck again.

14

After school, I was packing up my backpack at my locker when Dana came running up to me. "You aren't leaving, are you?"

I zipped the backpack shut. "Yes. Leaving," I said. "That's what I usually do after school."

Dana said something else, shouting over the loud voices in the crowded hall. I didn't hear her. I was watching a scene at the other end. Two girls held a boy by the arms while a third poured a bottle of water over his head.

"What is *that* about?" I asked.

Dana glanced over her shoulder as the boy grabbed the bottle away and began spraying it on the girls. She quickly turned back to me. "Freshmen," she muttered. "They're animals."

"Dana, what do you want?" I wasn't in a good mood. Lewis and I had a dumb fight in the lunchroom. I couldn't even remember what it was about. And then I discovered I'd done all the wrong problems for my Calc class.

Dana tugged my arm. "You can't go home, Jamie. You have to come to the gym. It's the team's last practice. You know. Before the tournament."

"No. I have my pottery class at the City Center," I said. "And I have to do my Calc homework all over again. I—"

"You *have* to come," Dana insisted. "The guys need a big send-off. A lot of kids are there already. Come on, Jamie. Do it for Clark, okay?"

Do it for Clark?

What was *Dana* doing for Clark last night? Hooking up with Nate?

"Okay, okay," I said. I glanced at my watch. "I'll stay a short while. I guess I can be a little late for pottery."

"Excellent!" She pulled me to the gym. "See you in a minute. I've got to round up some others."

I watched her run through the hall. Weird,

I thought. Since when does Dana get excited about sports? Before Clark, I don't think she knew a baseball bat from a hockey stick.

I pushed open the double doors to the gym. I was greeted by cheers from the bleachers and the thud of the basketball being dribbled up and down the court.

Clark waved to me as he dribbled slowly to the foul line. He stopped and sent up a high, floating jump shot. It hit the backboard and bounced off.

One of his teammates grabbed the rebound, dribbled around Clark, and passed to another player who made an easy layup.

I hurried across the floor to the bleachers on the other side of the gym. I saw twenty or thirty kids spread out on the metal benches, cheering the team, talking and laughing.

Four guys were huddled together at the top. They were passing a big bag of potato chips back and forth, not paying much attention to the practice.

Halfway up, I spotted Nate and Shark. Nikki sat one bench below them. Shark kept messing up her hair, and she slapped his hand away.

Aaron waved to me from the bottom bench. He sat with that girl I didn't know. I think she was a freshman.

Shifting my backpack on my shoulders, I climbed up the stairs and slid in next to Nikki.

"Jamie, looking good," Shark said. He reached down and squeezed my shoulders. "You look as awesome as I do. I can't believe you and I haven't hooked up yet!"

"Shark, are you crazy?" I cried. "Get your hands off me."

He tossed his head back and laughed.

Nikki jumped up and pretended to strangle him. "Shut up, Shark!" she cried. "You've been a total pain all afternoon."

He giggled.

Nikki, red-faced, dropped back onto the bench. "Ignore him," she muttered. "He thinks he's cute."

"How'd you get here so early from Waynesbridge?" I asked.

"They had to close the school," she said. "The furnace conked out. It was freezing. I couldn't hear my teachers because everyone's teeth was chattering!"

I laughed. Nikki had a great sense of humor.

Some cheers went up around us. One of the players must have done something good. I realized we weren't paying any attention to the practice.

I turned back to the floor. Clark caught a pass and jumped high with an easy layup. More cheers.

I saw Dana step into the gym. She stayed with her back against the double doors, her eyes on Clark.

I felt a sudden chill. I shut my eyes. The sound of the basketball thudding the hard-wood floor grew louder in my ears.

Whoa. I suddenly felt so weird.

My neck muscles tightened. I felt chill after chill ooze down my back.

I opened my eyes. The colors in the gym were all wrong. The players were all bright blue and red. The walls turned black.

What is happening to me?

I had the most powerful feeling of *dread*.

I jumped to my feet. I had to get away from there. I didn't know why. I just knew I had to hurry.

I saw Dana at the gym doors. The floor tilted one way, then the other as I tripped down the bleacher steps.

I made it to the gym floor. Wave after wave of dizziness rolled over me. I held both arms out to steady myself.

The players raced past me in a blur of blue and red. Wrong colors. Everything was wrong.

And then it lifted, as quickly as it had come over me.

The bright white gym lights returned. The walls shimmered white again. I felt my muscles loosen and relax.

What was *that* about?

Still walking unsteadily, I crossed the floor to Dana. I wanted to tell her I didn't feel well. I had to go home.

I was halfway across the floor when I heard a loud, metallic *crack*.

I heard a girl's cry.

Then another cracking sound, louder this time. A frightening *crunch*.

And then a rumbling noise, quickly drowned out by shrill screams.

With a gasp, I whipped around. I saw kids jumping up. Hands flew up in the air. Kids were diving and stumbling and falling.

Screams and cries.

I saw the potato chip bag sail down over the seats.

The whole world appeared to shake. The rumbling noise grew deafening until I covered my ears.

And opened my mouth in scream after scream as I realized the bleachers were collapsing.

15

Screams rose over the crack and crash of the falling metal. I watched helplessly as the four guys toppled backward off the top of the bleachers.

"Help me!"

"Look out!"

"What is happening?"

"Please—help!"

The panicked shouts forced me from my stupor. I darted forward to help—and saw the guys on the team running in front of me.

Clark and another kid had Nate by the arms. They were bent over the fallen benches, tugging him gently, all three of them talking at once. Nate grimaced, his eyes shut, his face twisted in pain.

The two boys freed Nate from the

wreckage. He shook himself and staggered forward. "My ankle—," he choked out. "I think it's broken."

Aaron and the freshman girl had been on the bottom bench. They jumped away when the bleachers started to collapse. Now they were working together, pulling kids out.

Kids were scattered over the gym floor, sprawling on their backs, huddled in small groups. Kids who were safe were crying and hugging one another.

"Shark? Where are you?" I called, finally finding my voice. But my words were drowned out by the shouts and cries from all around.

"Shark?"

The benches had crunched together. It looked like a ragged mountain of metal. I grabbed on to the edge of a low bench and started to pull myself up the bleachers.

I saw Shark above me. On his knees, waving to me.

"Are you okay?" I shouted, cupping my hands around my mouth.

"Yeah. Help me down," he replied. "I'm . . . dizzy, I guess. I feel shaky."

I took his hand and started to guide him down to the floor.

"*A curse on Shadyside High . . .*"

Nikki's words suddenly came back to me.

I heard sirens outside. Someone had called 911. Help was on the way.

"Is everyone out?" Coach Murphy was shouting, running frantically back and forth in front of the fallen bleachers. "Did everyone get out safe?"

Shark grabbed my arm. "Nikki!" he cried.

I searched the gym floor. I didn't see her.

"Nikki? Nikki?" Shark ran back to the bleachers, shouting her name. "Nikki? Where *are* you?"

I saw her before he did.

My hands shot up to my mouth to stop my scream.

I stared down into the bent metal. Stared at Nikki squeezed under the benches. Her arms pressed to her sides.

"Nikki? Nikki?"

I heard Shark's shouts somewhere to my left.

I started to wave frantically. But I couldn't speak.

I could only wave, my whole body trembling, and stare down at Nikki. Her face—crushed beneath the metal bench. Her face . . . crushed and broken.

Her skull smashed in. Blood running down her blond hair. One eyeball hanging loose.

Nikki. Crushed and broken. And dead.

PART THREE

16

Three days later. A dreary, cold afternoon, storm clouds low in the sky.

Dana and I were driving home after Nikki's funeral. It was held in a small chapel in Waynesbridge, too small for all the kids who showed up. A lot of us had to mill outside, unable to squeeze in for the ceremony.

We huddled together in the parking lot. It was totally awkward. No one knew what to say.

Now, I was glad Dana was driving. Because I couldn't stop crying. I didn't even know Nikki that well. But the horror of her death wouldn't leave me.

"They should have held it in a bigger place," Dana said, turning into a Wendy's. "You know. A big church or something."

I wiped my eyes. I was down to my last Kleenex. "Why are you turning in here?"

"I thought we'd get something to eat. Isn't that what people do after funerals? They eat?"

I sighed. My stomach felt as if it were filled with heavy rocks. But I followed her into the restaurant.

Dana ordered for both of us. It wasn't very crowded. Two little kids with their mother at one table. The kids were arguing over whose bag held the most French fries.

I found a booth at the back. I still had tears running down my cheeks. I pulled a few napkins from the dispenser and dried my eyes.

"Nikki's mother looked like she wouldn't survive the funeral," Dana said. "She couldn't stop sobbing. I guess she's all alone now. Nikki's dad lives in Florida, I think."

She unwrapped a cheeseburger and took a big bite. I struggled to pull the paper off my straw.

"Poor Shark," Dana murmured. "That's two for him, you realize."

I squinted at her. "Two? Huh?"

"Two girlfriends," Dana said. "First Candy died. Then Nikki."

I stared at her. I hadn't even thought of that.

She unwrapped my cheeseburger. "Jamie, you haven't eaten a thing all day. I watched you sit there at breakfast. Come on. Try to take a few bites."

I punched the straw through the lid on the Coke and took a sip. "It *isn't* a curse on Shadyside High," I said softly. "Nikki was wrong."

Dana tapped my hand. "What are you saying? Are you talking to yourself? I don't get you."

"Nikki said it was a curse on our school," I explained. "All the horrifying deaths. She said it was a curse on Shadyside. But . . . but . . ."

The tears came again. I just couldn't stop crying.

"But . . . she was wrong," I said finally. "Nikki didn't go to Shadyside. So you see? Dana, it's something *much worse*."

Dana's eyes went wide. She dropped her

cheeseburger onto its paper. "Ohmigod!" she cried.

I gasped. "Dana? Are you all right?"

"Ohmigod. Ohmigod," she repeated. She locked her eyes on mine. She suddenly looked totally pale.

"Dana—?"

"The brain is so weird," she said. "I just remembered something. I mean, it flashed into my brain, like, from out of nowhere. But it must have been in there this whole time."

"You're not making a lot of sense," I said. "Why don't you take a deep breath and—"

"No. I'm making sense," she insisted. "I . . . just remembered something that happened. In your garage, Jamie. That night I faced Angelica Fear."

"Oh." I shuddered. "What happened?"

Dana covered her mouth with one hand. "Oh, wow. It just came back to me. I must have shoved it away because it's so frightening."

"What?" I demanded. "What *is* it?"

Dana locked her dark eyes on me again. "Angelica told me why she was killing everyone. She *told* me, Jamie. She said she came back to life because she wanted to kill all the kids who went inside the Fear Mansion before it was torn down. All the kids who discovered her secret room."

Dana took a deep breath. "She said the kids who found her secret room *looted* it. They took her possessions. And now she planned to kill them all."

I shuddered again. I realized I'd stopped breathing the whole time Dana was talking. Now I let my breath out in a long whoosh.

"Dana," I whispered. "We *all* were there. Lewis and Shark and Nate and me and . . . and . . . We *all* were there that night. We *all* took things. Every one of us."

Her mouth dropped open. She didn't reply.

My mind was spinning. The bright lights in the restaurant shimmered in my eyes. I shut them, struggling to think clearly.

"Angelica Fear must still be around," I murmured. "She killed Nikki. Nikki was there that night. Ada . . . Whitney . . . Everyone who died. They were there that night. They stole stuff from Angelica's secret room."

I opened my eyes. "Oh, wow, Dana. Don't you see? Angelica is still around. And she wants to kill the rest of us. We're *all* in horrible danger!"

That night, I couldn't sleep. I sat up in bed, drenched in sweat. The clock on my bed table said 1:13.

Angelica is going to kill us all, I thought, hugging myself. And I'm the only one who knows it.

I climbed to my feet. I have to find her. I have to stop her somehow.

I crept across my room, stepping through a pool of pale moonlight on the floor. My hands trembling, I slid open the bottom dresser drawer. I fumbled around in the back until I found the bracelet. Then I slipped it over my right wrist.

"Angelica, are you here?" I whispered. "Are you here?"

17

Silence.

A silence that rang in my ears.

No. No reply from Angelica.

I shivered. Was she there in my room watching me? Teasing me by not answering?

I knew I couldn't sleep. Maybe I'd never sleep again!

I pulled on jeans and a couple of sweaters. Then I sneaked downstairs, out of the house, and began walking through the chilled darkness to Nights.

Lewis. Lewis will cheer me up, I told myself.

Lewis will hold me and assure me that I'm okay. That we're not all in some kind of horrifying nightmare. That no hundred-year-old ghost plans to kill us all.

My heart was pounding by the time I turned onto Fear Street. My breath puffed up in front of me.

The world seemed even more still than usual. Nothing moved, not a blade of grass on the dew-crusted lawns, not even the few leaves left hanging on the trees.

Silence.

My throat suddenly ached. I started to jog faster. I needed the warmth of the bar. The friendly faces. Lewis.

The silver bracelet bounced on my wrist. I jammed my icy hands into my parka pockets.

Squinting into the gray dimness, I watched for the lights of the Fear Street Acres shopping center. To my surprise, I saw only darkness up ahead.

My first thought: It must be foggier than I realized. The lights must be hidden behind thick fog.

My second thought: Has a power blackout turned off all the lights?

I jogged across the street. Then stopped.

No lights on at Nights? Had Ryland closed up tonight?

A wave of panic swept over me. I spun around. No streetlights behind me. No glow of red or green from the traffic light at Fear and Walker.

Whoa.

Where is the bar?

I took a deep, shuddering breath and moved forward. "Hey, anyone here?" I shouted. "Anyone?" My voice came out high and shrill.

I let out a gasp as I realized I was staring up a dark hill. A steeply sloping lawn, stretching all gray and black under the pale sliver of moonlight.

I'm on the wrong block, I decided.

I made a wrong turn.

But, no. I turned back and glimpsed the tilted street sign at the corner. Fear Street. Yes. Here I was.

But the lights? The shopping center? The bar?

All darkness. Shadows swaying over the

sloping lawn. And at the top of the hill . . .

An enormous house, all blacks and purples. Hunkering up there like a giant animal about to pounce.

The slanted roofs. The twin chimneys on either side, rising beside castlelike turrets. The balconies and terraces.

Of course I recognized it.

Of course I knew what house I was staring at in such trembling horror.

But how could I believe it?

How could I believe my own eyes?

For I was staring up at the Fear Mansion. The house that was torn down nearly two years ago.

I had been there that day. Lewis and I had watched it come down.

All of the old mansions on Fear Street were destroyed—blown up, knocked down, and carted away—to make way for the shopping center.

But now I stood at the bottom of the lawn, my hands jammed into my pockets, my body shuddering in disbelief, gazing up at the mansion. Not a burned-out shell as I remembered it. But tall and whole, as it must have looked a hundred years ago.

"No. It ... can't be," I stammered out loud. And then I cupped my hands around my mouth and started to shout. "Is anybody here? Can anybody *help* me?"

No. No reply.

And then I felt the push at my back. The strong push forcing me up the hill, my shoes slipping on the frosted ground, the tall grass matted down and frozen.

I felt something—or someone—pushing me to the house.

I opened my mouth to cry once again for help. But this time, no sound came out. My breath caught in my throat. My heart seemed to leap in my chest.

Something drew me forward.

Pushed me, tugged me toward the old house.

The old house that *couldn't* be there!

Was it some kind of evil Fear magic?

Was this Angelica's revenge?

I couldn't breathe. I straightened my legs, tightened my muscles, pushed my heels into the hard ground. Struggled to resist, to fight back against the invisible force.

But now the wide columns of the front

porch loomed over me. And the thick wood of the double front doors creaked as the doors slowly swung open.

Beyond them, I saw eerie green light, thick and foggy, a billowing light.

Closer . . . closer.

"No! Please—please!" I finally found my voice. "Help me, somebody! Stop! Stop! Please!"

I couldn't fight it. I couldn't stop myself.

"Somebody—please?"

A strong push sent me stumbling inside. The heavy doors slammed hard behind me.

18

The slam of the door echoed like thunder through the enormous house. I heard wave after wave of sound, as if I were standing at the ocean shore.

I took a deep breath and tried to stop my shivering. The air inside the house carried a heavy chill, colder than the air outside. I gasped as I felt a stab of cold on my skin, as if an icy hand had gripped the back of my neck.

The green fog swirled around me, billowing thickly, rising and falling. Beyond it, I could see what appeared to be a couch and chairs—dark, heavy furniture arranged in front of a dead fireplace.

I turned to the door, eager to escape. But I could no longer see it through the heavy, green snakes of fog. Dark doorways seemed to pop up around me. Doorway after doorway, until I shut my eyes, wishing them to disappear.

I stumbled forward, bumping my knee on a low ottoman.

"Ohh!" I cried out, grabbing the back of a leather couch to keep from falling.

The furniture felt real, heavy and solid.

But how *could* it be real?

How could I be standing in the Fear Mansion two years after it had been torn down?

Gripping the back of the couch, I held my breath and listened. Did I hear the soft shuffle of shoes on carpet? Was someone in here with me?

Angelica Fear?

"No—!" I uttered a low cry. Pushed myself away from the couch. Bolted forward, into the nearest doorway. And found myself in a library, dark books shelved from floor to ceiling on all sides.

Where is the front door?

I spun away and hurtled myself through the next door. It opened onto a long, narrow hall, completely black. I could hear the rush of wind through the passageway. Or was that my own shallow breathing?

I knew I had to get out of that house. Before I went totally crazy, I had to find the front door. Or any door that would lead to escape!

I darted back into the swirling curtains of green mist. The fog circled me, held me prisoner, spun me around until I stumbled in total dizziness.

Finally, gathering all my strength, I lowered my shoulders, ducked my head, and burst forward, breaking through the mist. Breaking free!

But where was I now? In another entryway surrounded by dark, empty doorways.

"Is anyone here? Is anyone here?" I didn't even realize I was crying out. My voice came out hollow and dull, and echoed off the walls.

"Anyone here?"

I darted frantically from door to door, peering into dark, empty rooms.

And then a flickering, orange light caught my eye. I stopped, my heart pounding. And crept to the doorway.

Another library? Or was it the same one I'd seen before?

My gaze fell over a wall of dark books. Two brown leather couches facing each other. A long table stacked with papers.

I raised my eyes to the wide stone fireplace. The flickering light came from a log fire, crackling quietly.

I squinted into the dancing flames. I realized I was staring at a fire in a house that didn't exist.

I took a step back. My mind whirred. This was too weird. No matter how much I struggled, there was no way I could make sense of it.

And then I saw something move. A man!

He stood up slowly from the couch. He had his back to me. Outlined in the flickering flames, he wore a dark suit. His hair was long.

I grabbed the door frame, unable to move, unable to breathe.

He turned slowly, and his face came into view. I saw dark eyes, a slender, weary face.

And I recognized him.

Yes, I recognized him at once.

19

I wanted to scream. I wanted to hide.

I wanted to shut my eyes and wake up in my own bed, far away from this nightmare.

But there I stood, my whole body trembling. Afraid to breathe, afraid to make a sound.

There I stood, gazing at the dark figure in front of the fire. *Staring at Simon Fear.*

Yes, I recognized him from the bronze plaque on the wall at Nights. And I knew him from a dozen old photographs I'd seen while studying the Fear family.

Of course he'd been dead for nearly a hundred years.

Of course his house had been destroyed, replaced by the bar my friends and I hung out in and the shopping center around it.

Of course . . . of course.

In my terror, I couldn't try to reason this out. My mind was frozen now, frozen in horror.

I had only one thought: to escape.

To get out of that house before he saw me.

I watched him step toward the fire. He held out his hands to the flames.

With a sharp intake of breath, I spun away from the doorway and started to run. My shoes thudded on the hard wood, echoing loudly down the long halls. But I didn't care. I had to run. I had to find the way out.

And there they were. The double front doors, one of them still open a crack.

I took off, running full speed now, my sides aching, my chest about to burst. Out the door, onto the porch, into the cold, fresh air. I didn't slow my pace. Slipping and sliding on the frosty ground, I tore down the hill and kept running.

I was nearly a block away when I turned and glanced back. The house still rose up darkly over the hill. And in one window, I could see the blinking yellow firelight.

"Lewis."

I said his name out loud as I started to jog toward his house.

Lewis was the only one who would understand, the only one who would *believe* me.

Normally, I'd look for him at Nights. But there *was* no Nights!

The world had gone back in time. The world had gone crazy.

The world had turned into a nightmare, and I knew Lewis was the only one I could turn to.

His new house was nearly a mile away. I wanted to go home and get the car. But I was afraid of waking my parents. So I half-jogged, half-ran the whole way.

Through the still night. The houses dark. No cars on the street.

About a block from Lewis's house, I saw headlights sweep over the street. A patrol car rolled slowly across the intersection. I sank back, pressing up against a hedge, eager not to be seen.

Try explaining *my* night to a cop!

"You see, Officer, the Fear Mansion suddenly came back, and I went inside, and . . ."

Yeah, sure.

I waited until the patrol car was out of

sight. Then I pushed away from the hedge and, walking now, made my way to Lewis's house.

The front of the house was dark. But I saw orange light seeping from under the blinds in the last window. Lewis's room.

I hurried up to the window. The new sod had just been put down, and chunks of it were still loose. I grabbed on to the windowsill and tapped my fist against the glass.

I waited. Then tapped again.

Come on, Lewis. Come on! I need you!

After a minute or two, the blinds pulled up. Lewis peered out at me, surprise on his face, his hair matted to his forehead.

He pulled open the window. "Jamie? What's wrong?"

"Plenty," I said. "Please—let me in. I . . . I have to talk to you."

He brushed back his hair, blinking himself awake. Then he slid the window open further. He reached out, grabbed me under the arms, and helped pull me into his room.

I found my balance, but didn't let go of him. I wrapped my arms around his T-shirt and held on tight, pressing my cheek against his.

"Hey, you're cold," I said. "Have you been outside?"

He shook his head. "No. I was asleep." He straightened his shirt collar. "What's wrong, Jamie? What are you doing here?"

I just blurted it out. "The Fear Mansion is back." I held on to his hands. They were both cold too.

He narrowed his eyes at me. "Excuse me? I . . . don't get it."

"It's back," I repeated. "Believe me. Please believe me, Lewis." My voice broke. I threw my arms around him again and hugged him. We stood there like that for a long time.

Then he led me over to his bed, and we sat side by side, holding hands.

"Start at the beginning," he said softly.

"It's not a long story," I said. "I couldn't sleep, so I walked to Nights. I thought maybe you'd be there. But . . . but . . . everything was dark, Lewis. I mean . . ."

The words caught in my throat. I swallowed and started again.

"Fear Street Acres—it was gone. Nights, too. It was all dark. And the old hill was back.

And the house . . . the Fear Mansion. It was back. And I went inside. I mean, something pulled me in, and—"

"Whoa. Wait." He put his fingers over my lips to silence me. "Look at you," he said. "You're a total mess. You're out of breath and—" He stared hard at me. "Did you run all the way here?"

"You're not listening to me!" I screamed. "Don't you hear what I'm telling you? The Fear Mansion is back! And inside it, I . . . I saw Simon Fear."

He squeezed my hands. He slid the bracelet back and forth on my wrist. "I'm worried about you," he murmured, avoiding my eyes. "Maybe we should call your parents or something."

"No, Lewis, please—," I pleaded.

"Ssshh." Again, he placed a finger gently over my mouth. "Calm. Take a deep breath, Jamie. And listen to what you're telling me. You know the Fear Mansion can't be back. It's impossible. No way you could go inside a house that was knocked down."

He let go of the bracelet. "You and I

watched them knock it down—remember?"

I pulled free of him and jumped to my feet. "I'm not crazy!" I screamed.

He jumped up beside me. "You'll wake my parents! Just keep it down, okay?"

"I'm not crazy," I repeated, lowering my voice. "I'll prove it to you."

"Huh? Prove that the Fear Mansion is back?" He reached for me, but I backed away. "You've been totally stressed out, Jamie," he said. "I'm really worried. I think you need help now. I—"

"Get dressed," I said.

He squinted at me.

"Get dressed. I'll take you there," I said. "You can see with your own eyes. Then maybe you'll believe me."

A chill ran down my back. I hadn't removed my parka. I burrowed inside it and shoved my hands deep into the pockets.

A few minutes later, we silently backed Lewis's mother's car out of the garage and down to the street. We climbed in and started the engine. But we didn't turn on the headlights until we were in the next block.

We'd learned a lot about sneaking out during our two years of going to Nights. We were experts. So far, none of us had been caught. Our parents were all clueless.

Lewis and I drove to Fear Street in silence. He tapped his fingers on the wheel and kept his eyes straight ahead.

I hit the passenger door when he swerved to avoid a trash can that had rolled into the street. "You okay?" he asked, straightening the wheel.

"Yeah. Okay," I said. He had the heater up full blast, and the hot air felt good against my face.

"Lewis, it's back," I said, gazing out into the darkness. "I don't know how or why. But it's back. It's some kind of evil magic. From Angelica Fear. I know it. I'm not crazy."

He let out a long sigh. "I want to believe you. I really do," he said. "But . . ." His voice trailed off.

He slowed the car. He pointed out the windshield.

I followed his gaze and saw the lights up ahead. White pinpricks against the night sky.

The lights grew brighter as the car approached. The store windows sharpened into focus.

The windows of Fear Street Acres.

Lewis pulled the car to the curb and stopped. We both stared out at Nights Bar.

"Oh—" A muffled cry escaped my lips. And then I collapsed. Just broke down. And started to cry.

"It's okay," Lewis whispered. He put his arms around me and drew me to him. "It's okay, Jamie. It'll all be okay."

He held me and let me cry on his shoulder.

"It's okay," he repeated. "I'll take care of you. I really will."

20

Well, that was an adventure last night. The poor girl had quite a fright. Imagine seeing a house that had been gone for two years. Being forced inside by some invisible hand and—most frightening of all—setting eyes on Simon Fear!

Dear dead Simon. Dear dead ME.

Jamie was so busy obsessing about Angelica, she never guessed it was me all along. She doesn't know that I am young and alive again. Having my fun messing with Jamie's mind, as they say today.

She's in my power now. It was so easy to arrange. Almost too easy.

The power, of course, is in the bracelet. Did she really think I stole it for her just to please her?

It was so easy to have her find that bracelet in the flea market. She has no idea of its powers, no idea of how I can use it to control her mind, her actions—her whole world.

She's terribly frightened and confused now. And of course she blames Angelica.

Fine. Fine. The more she blames my poor dead wife, the further away she'll be from the truth.

It's a laugh, isn't it?

But I think I've had enough fun teasing Jamie. I have serious work to do.

Time for the blood to flow.

I won't rest until the blood flows and my revenge is complete.

Now she will meet the real Fear.

PART FOUR

21

"Lewis, what are you smiling about?" I asked.

He kept his eyes on the road ahead. His smile grew wider. "It's a secret smile," he said.

The houses of Shadyside gave way to woods, then wide, empty farm fields. Through the car window, I could see the tiny dots of white stars in the purple-black sky. A clear, cold night.

I smoothed my gloved hand over Lewis's coat sleeve. "Are you keeping secrets from me?"

"Plenty," he replied. "That's why it's a secret smile."

I gave him a gentle shove. "You're weird tonight."

His smile faded. "This whole night is

weird. A bonfire at Miller's Farm in March?"

"It's a pep rally," I said.

"Isn't it a little cold for a pep rally?" He swerved around a dead raccoon in the highway.

"You're such a wimp," I said. I pinched his cheek. "Afraid your little toesies will get cold?"

He grabbed my glove and squeezed it. "Will you warm them up for me later?"

I pulled my hand back to my lap. "Maybe."

"Why can't they have the pep rally in May or June?" he asked.

"Because there's no basketball tournament in May or June. Duh." The heater in his mom's car wasn't sending out much hot air. I pulled my wool ski cap down further on my head.

"You know, this is kinda exciting," I said. "I mean, Shadyside hasn't gone to the tournament in years. That's why we've never had a winter pep rally."

An arrow-shaped wooden sign read: MILLER'S FARM. Lewis turned the car onto a long, gravel drive. The tires skidded on the slick gravel.

Up ahead, I could see rows of cars and

SUVs parked on the grass. Torches on long poles sent up flames of yellow-orange light. The torches led to a field in front of the barn, where lots of kids had already gathered.

Lewis slowed the car and pulled it up beside the last parked car. "What's up with your cousin Dana?" Lewis said. "She's totally psyched about this."

I nodded. "Dana the cheerleader," I said. "Can you believe that?"

I pushed open the passenger door, climbed out, and took a deep breath of the cold, fresh air. I could smell straw and grass and cows and dirt—farm smells.

My cousin Cindy lived on a farm outside Shadyside when we were little kids. I used to stay with her every summer. She flashed into my mind as I started toward the field. I had this picture of the two of us running through the cornfields late at night, a big full moon hanging right over our heads.

"Hey, Jamie!" Dana's shout interrupted my thoughts. She came running up to us, her coat open and flapping behind her as she ran. "I've been calling you. Didn't you hear me?"

"Dana, hi," I said. "What's up?"

"Check it out." Dana pointed to the pile of wood and straw stretching up as high as the barn roof. "We've been building the bonfire all afternoon," she said. "Look at me. I'm covered in dust and dirt."

She wiped her forehead with the back of one hand. "It's going to be an awesome fire," she said, taking me by the arm and pulling me toward the field.

"Hey—I'm here too!" Lewis said, running to my other side and taking my other arm.

The ground crunched beneath our shoes. A strong gust of wind flattened the tall grass and made a soft, whistling sound.

I heard kids singing an old U2 song. Two boys were wrestling on the ground in front of the bonfire pile, and a crowd gathered to watch.

Some coaches hurried to break it up. But it wasn't a fight. The guys were just goofing.

We were nearing the end of the parking lot when I saw Galen and Aaron. They stood between two SUVs. Aaron had a brown paper bag in his hand. He passed it to Galen.

"Hey, Jamie," Galen called, waving us over. "Wine?"

Lewis laughed. "You guys got wine?" He took the paper bag from Aaron and sniffed it.

"My parents weren't home," Galen said. "They won't miss it."

Lewis handed me the bottle. I took a taste. Some kind of red wine. It felt very warm and soothing as it went down.

Dana glanced around nervously. "You guys could get suspended for this, you know."

Aaron tilted the bottle to his mouth and drank.

"It's cold," Galen said, grinning at Dana. "We're just trying to stay warm."

"The fire will warm you up," Dana said. "It's going to be enormous!" She pointed. "We found all these old rotting boards inside the barn. They're going to burn like crazy."

"Hey, there's Lissa," Aaron said. He tossed the paper bag to Galen and took off, running to greet the red-haired girl I'd seen with him before.

"Aaron's in love," Galen said, snickering.

He finished the bottle and tossed it under the SUV.

"Who is she?" I asked. "Where's she from?"

Galen shrugged. "Mars, I think."

Dana pulled me away. "Come on, guys. It's going to start."

Galen grinned at Dana. "Where's your cheerleader outfit?"

"Hope you're not making fun of me," Dana shot back. "Because I can take you, Galen." She shook a fist at him.

Galen squinted at her, trying to focus. I could see he'd drunk a lot of wine. He tottered a little as he stepped up to Dana. "You want a piece of me? Want to take this outside?"

Lewis pulled him back. "We're *already* outside, dude."

"Oh. Yeah." He turned to Dana. "Want to kiss and make up?"

Dana made a disgusted face. "Kiss *you*? Are you *crazy*?" She took off, running toward the circle of kids in front of the barn.

Galen squinted at me. "Was that a no?"

We made our way past tall bales of straw piled up in bunches of three and four. Another wind gust sent dust and bits of straw swirling in the air.

I saw Nate and Shark at the back of the circle. Shark was perched on a low straw bale. Nate leaned against it, talking rapidly to Shark, moving his hands as he talked. Shark laughed and tossed a handful of straw in Nate's face.

One of the coaches stepped up to the portable microphone system. In the darting light from the torches, I couldn't see who it was.

I gazed up at the tower ready for the bonfire. Along with tons of lumber and newspapers and sticks and straw, old chairs and a beat-up wreck of a couch had been tossed on the pile.

The tower must have been twenty or thirty feet tall, taller than the barn. How did they ever build it? I wondered. It will make an amazing fire, I thought.

The wind gusts made a rattling sound as they blew against the tall pile. Behind us, the barn doors creaked.

A wall of straw bales stood against the barn. From somewhere behind the barn, I heard the low *hoot hoot* of a barn owl.

Lewis slid his arm around my shoulders. We huddled close together at the back of the circle and watched.

Coach Murphy struggled to get everyone quiet. Finally, he started to give a short speech. The loudspeaker kept squealing, and no one seemed to be able to stop it. Finally, the coach tossed the mike down in disgust and shouted his talk.

Then the cheerleading squad ran into the middle of the circle and led everyone in four or five cheers. "Tigers roar! Tigers roar! Tigers roar! Tigers SCORE!"

At first, only a few kids joined in. But after a few cheers, everyone forgot about being cool and started to get into the spirit of the thing.

Lewis and I aren't rah-rah-types. Especially since we're older than everyone. We would have graduated last year if it hadn't been for our accident. But we started cheering too.

Dana was jumping up and down. She cheered the loudest when Clark was introduced. Clark brought a basketball and he tossed it high into the crowd. That got a game going as kids started heaving the ball back and forth across the circle.

Lots of laughing and kidding around. Someone broke into a totally obscene version of the school fight song, and everyone joined in.

Coach Murphy waved his hands and shouted, trying to get the singing stopped. Finally, kids began chanting, "Fire! Fire! Fire!"

The cheerleaders dipped torches in buckets of kerosene and lit them. They stood in a line, holding the flaming torches high. The wind made the flames dance and shimmy.

Lewis tapped me on the shoulder. "They're selling hot cider over there." He pointed to a table near the barn entrance. "I'm going to get a cup. You want some?"

"Sure," I said. "Thanks."

He trotted off toward the barn. I turned back to the cheerleaders with their flaming torches. "Everybody, back five steps! Back five steps!" Coach Murphy shouted.

"This fire is going to *rock*!" Dana declared.

"Go, Tigers!" some kids yelled. "Burn the Red Hawks!"

"Burn the Red Hawks! Burn the Red Hawks!" The chant spread quickly around the circle.

"Back five paces!" Coach Murphy bellowed.

We all obediently moved back across the wet grass.

And then a hush fell over the crowd as the cheerleaders formed a circle around the tall tower. They lowered their torches and set the pile ablaze on all sides at once.

A cheer rose up over the field as the wood flamed up . . . slowly at first, and then crackling flames climbed up the sides. The old couch caught. Big tufts of straw lit up, tossing in the wind.

The fire shot up the tall structure, rising like a rocket, crackling, popping, darting out in all directions.

"It's beautiful!" Dana declared, slapping me a hard high five.

I had to agree with her. I'd never seen such an awesome column of bright fire rising up to the sky. It looked like some kind of movie special effects.

And just as I thought that, I saw the tower start to tilt.

My mouth dropped open as the tower bent . . . bent . . . then toppled over.

I pressed my hands to my face, unable to scream.

With a rumble that sounded like thunder, the flaming straw and boards and chairs and chunks of wood came falling, falling over everyone, the flames leaping out, shooting over the ground.

Screams rose up over the roar of the fire.

I saw kids running, their coats on fire. Rolling in the dew-wet grass. Balls of red-yellow fire bounced over the ground—like Clark's basketball. The fireballs fell from the sky, bouncing over the hard ground.

I saw a bale of straw catch flame. And then another.

And now the structure had completely fallen and lay across the field, flaming, shooting up streaks of fire, spreading over the field, a hot, burning wall of dancing flame.

I grabbed Dana, who stared straight ahead, frozen in shock. The two of us stumbled back as blast after blast of heat washed over us.

I let out a cry when I saw the barn catch in a fiery whoosh of flame, so loud, it sounded like an explosion. And now the barn roof burned, sending up another high wall of leaping flames. And fire burst from the front wall of the barn.

It all went up so fast.

The barn. The bales of straw. The lumber and . . .

And . . .

I saw the owls flying up from the barn. The owls with their wings on fire. Flames darted over their backs as they flapped up against the night sky, screeching, screeching out their pain.

"The owls are burning!" someone screamed. "The owls are burning!"

I turned away and covered my ears. I couldn't bear to watch. "Lewis—?" I called. I wanted him to hold me. But I didn't see him.

Dana held on to my sleeve. "Lewis? Where is he?" She gazed behind me, then turned and glanced all around.

"Lewis?" I repeated, my eyes searching the

faces of fleeing, screaming kids, faces so bright and unnatural, so horrifyingly bright surrounded by the walls of fire.

"Where is he?" Dana repeated, not letting go of me.

"He . . . went to get cider," I managed to say. "Over there. By the barn."

I couldn't see the cider table. Was it that thing on fire by the barn door? Did Lewis get trapped in the fire?

"Lewis?"

I pulled free of Dana's grasp and took off, running to the flames, cupping my hands around my mouth and screaming the whole way.

"Lewis? Lewis?"

22

"Lewis? Lewis—?"

My screams were drowned out by the shrieks and wails of other terrified kids. We all seemed to be running in frantic circles, calling out one another's names, shouting for help as the flames shot out, attacked, pulled back, and spread.

"Lewis—?"

Someone bumped me hard from behind, and I fell to my knees. I pulled myself up quickly.

Kids ran past me, stampeding to safety.

A deafening explosion of sound swept over me, making the ground shake. I saw the barn roof collapse under a roaring wall of flames.

"Hey! Jamie!" Shark grabbed my arm. His

eyes were wide, and I could see fire reflected in them. "You okay?"

I nodded.

"Shark, have you seen Lewis?" I asked, my voice high and shrill. "I can't find Lewis." I shivered. Despite the cold of the night, sweat poured down my forehead.

Shark shook his head. He looked dazed. "Nate was right next to me," he said. "And Aaron and Galen and that girl. Have you seen them? Where did they go?"

"I . . . I don't know," I said. "I'm looking for Lewis. He went over by the barn and—"

I stopped. Outlined by orange flames, I saw Lewis running toward us.

"Over here!" I screamed. "Over here!"

I ran to him. Hugged him. Pressed his hot face against mine. "You're okay?"

He nodded, brushing back his hair. "I was at the side of the barn when the tower fell. I just took off. Like a shot. I knew the barn would catch."

"I . . . was worried," I said, holding on to him. "Where did you run? Why didn't you run back to me?"

"I was helping the cheerleaders," Lewis said. "They were standing right under the tower when it fell. One of them got burned pretty badly. Kristen Blake. I think the rest are okay."

I heard the rise and fall of sirens in the distance. Someone must have called 911.

"There's Nate over there with Coach Murphy," Shark said. He grabbed Lewis's arm. "Did you see Aaron? Galen? Were they over by the barn?"

Lewis shook his head. "I don't know. Let's look for them."

We took off, jogging together. The wind blew thick, black smoke over us. I tried to cover my eyes, but the smoke burned my nostrils and choked my throat. All three of us started to cough.

I turned my back against the wind. The flames covered the barn now, leaping high into the night sky, making the ground as bright as day.

Sirens blaring, red lights flashing on their roofs, ambulances rolled onto the grass, followed by a line of fire trucks. The shrill sirens competed with the screams and cries.

Shielding my eyes, I spun around. The whole field appeared to be on fire. Blades of burning straw floated in the air, carried on the smoke-filled wind.

More ambulances and fire trucks rumbled onto the grass. Near the gravel drive, I spotted Clark and Dana. Clark had his arm around her shoulders. Her dark hair was blowing wild above her face. The two of them stood motionless, staring at the fiery horror on the farm field.

"Aaron? Galen?" Shark shouted their names.

Dozens of kids were running to the parking lot, escaping. Some ran with cell phones to their ears, probably calling home, telling their parents what had happened and that they were okay.

The field was emptying out.

Shark, Lewis, and I ducked low and darted between two flaming bales of straw. The blast of heat made my skin burn.

"Aaron? Galen?"

I had to close my eyes because of another thick cloud of smoke. Lewis held my arm and pulled me over the grass.

When I opened my eyes, I saw that we were nearly to the fence at the end of the field. The sirens and shouts and voices were far behind us.

I blinked. Two shadowy forms up ahead didn't move.

Scarecrows?

Why would the farm have scarecrows up in an empty field at the end of winter?

"Oh, no," Lewis muttered. I heard the fear in his voice. "No. Oh, no."

The scarecrows tilted on tall poles.

The three of us ducked through the fence and made our way closer.

"Oh—!" A soft cry escaped my throat, and I grabbed Lewis's arm.

I stared at the two figures dangling on the poles.

Not scarecrows.

Not scarecrows.

Aaron and Galen, tilting toward each other. Hanging limp and lifeless on the poles.

Their mouths and ears, their shirts and pants—stuffed with straw.

23

"Maybe we should stop coming to Nights," Nate said.

Shark groaned. He raised his beer bottle to his mouth and drained it. "Why should we have to give up our secret life?" he said, shaking his head. "We didn't do anything wrong."

"There's a murderer out there," Nate said, looking pale and frightened in the dim light of the bar. "He's murdering our friends one by one, Shark. Maybe it's not safe for us to be sitting here in the middle of the night. Maybe we're sitting ducks."

"Quack quack," Shark said without smiling. He signaled Ryland to bring him another Budweiser.

It was a week later, a week after the horrible fire and murders at the pep rally. The principal had pulled the basketball team out of the tournament. The high school was closed for three days. Counselors were available for any kids who wanted to talk to them.

The police questioned us all, everyone who had been at Miller's Farm that night. No one had seen anyone suspicious lurking around the field or barn. No one had seen *anything* that might help the police find the murderer.

Of course, Dana and I knew the murderer couldn't be found.

The murderer was a hundred-year-old ghost. Or maybe *two* hundred-year-old ghosts.

Dana and I knew why Aaron and Galen died. We were the *only* ones who knew.

And what we knew was driving us crazy.

No way we could explain it to the police. Or our parents. Or even our friends.

We hardly believed it ourselves.

In the days after the bonfire, I moved between dark clouds of shock and anger. Sometimes my world was a total blur. I couldn't think straight. I couldn't see straight.

Mom saw the trouble I was in. She wanted to take me to Dr. Fineman, our family doctor.

I argued her out of it. I knew he'd be useless.

"Dr. Fineman, my friends are all being killed by Simon and Angelica Fear. I know they've been dead for a century. But they came back to murder all of us who broke into their house last year."

Yeah. For sure.

Jamie has gone Looney Tunes.

When I wasn't lost in a haze, I felt only anger, the strongest, bitterest anger I'd ever felt in my life.

How could this happen to me and my friends?

It was so unfair. So tragic and unfair.

And who would be next? Would it be *me*?

Dana's way of dealing with it? She shoved it all aside. I don't know how she did it. But most of the time, she swept it to the back of her mind.

Was it because she'd had so many other bad things happen in her life?

I couldn't explain it. I guess I admired her for being able to go on as if things were almost normal.

I couldn't do it.

So we all gathered at Nights to talk talk talk. All the Night People. Trying to talk our way through the horror. Trying to explain it away somehow.

Everyone wants to wake up from a nightmare. But what if the nightmare refuses to go away?

We'd pulled our chairs together at the back of the bar. No separate tables anymore. We knew we were all in this together.

Shark and Nate, grim-faced, baseball caps pulled down over their foreheads, sat together in one corner. I kept thinking there should be a chair for Nikki. But of course she would not be arriving.

Clark had his arm around Dana. He kept leaning against her and whispering in her ear. Dana kept glancing over to me.

For some reason, Lewis seemed very distant tonight. He sat away from me, across from Shark and Nate. And he didn't say much. He sipped a Diet Coke and kept staring at the neon Budweiser sign at the front of the bar, as if hypnotized.

"I heard a rumor that Kristen Blake's

parents are suing the school," Clark said. "You know. For negligence. Because of her burns."

"Lotsa rumors going around," Lewis muttered without looking at anyone.

"Don't you think Aaron's parents will sue?" Shark said. "And Galen's?"

"Sue who?" Nate said. "Sue the murderer?"

"Coach Murphy may get canned," Clark said. "That's totally unfair."

"Nobody holds him responsible—do they?" Dana asked. She glanced at me. She knew who was really responsible.

It was so hard not to stand up and just blurt out the truth. But I knew I couldn't. I didn't want them to think I was crazy.

I didn't want them to know I'd been inhabited by Angelica Fear. No way. I didn't want them to know I'd gone back into the Fear Mansion. I'd seen Simon Fear.

Hel-lo. Who would believe a story like that?

Was I being a coward by not revealing the truth? Or was I being brave, keeping it to myself?

"We're all that's left," Shark muttered, motioning with his head. "Just the six of us." He spun his beer bottle between his hands.

"The last of the Night People," Nate said, eyes lowered to the floor. He sighed. "This used to be so much fun. All of us sneaking out at night, having the whole town just to ourselves."

"Clark and I weren't here when you guys started doing this," Dana said. "Jamie told me you started out meeting inside the Fear Mansion. Before it was torn down."

Hel-lo. Was *that* why Dana was handling all of this better than I was? Because she knew she and Clark weren't there the night we looted the Fear Mansion?

Did she feel safe? Did she think Angelica's revenge had nothing to do with her?

In a way, I hoped she was right. I didn't want any harm to come to my cousin.

I didn't want any harm to come to any of us.

Suddenly, as they chattered on, I knew what I had to do.

I jumped to my feet. I turned and hurried toward the front door.

"Jamie—?" I heard Lewis call.

"Where are you going?" Dana shouted.

"Home," I said. I pushed open the door and stepped out into a cold, clear night.

Yes. Clear. Suddenly it all became clear to me.

I couldn't sit around drinking beer and talking about how sad I was and let Simon or Angelica or whoever kill us one by one. I had to do something.

This all started at the Fear Mansion. And I knew it had to end at the Fear Mansion. . . .

24

"I'm the only one who can stop the killings," I told myself.

Four o'clock in the morning. Solid blackness outside my window. The only light in my room—the tiny bulb in my desk lamp against the wall.

I was still dressed. I'd pulled off my shoes so my parents wouldn't hear me walking around. When I passed his room, I heard my little brother Danny coughing in his sleep.

He had a cold. No big deal.

I wondered if the little guy knew about the murders in my class. The story was all over the news. It was the only thing people in Shadyside talked about. I wondered if Danny and his friends frightened one another by talking about it too.

My cell had rung all the way home in the car from Nights. I glanced at the screen: Lewis. He kept calling and calling, but I didn't pick up.

I knew what I had to do. And it didn't involve Lewis.

Now the phone started to ring again. I pressed it off before it woke up Danny or my parents. Lewis certainly was being persistent.

I guessed he was just worried about me.

Well . . . I was worried about me too.

I pulled the bracelet from my dresser drawer. The blue jewels gleamed dully in the dim light.

I gazed at the bracelet as I slid it onto my wrist. It felt smooth and cool against my skin.

Was it really Angelica Fear's?

Did it have powers?

It had the same design as Angelica's amulet. Did it also have the same magic?

I hoped so.

My plan was to use the magic. To confront Angelica or Simon—or both of them. To face them. To defeat them. To stop the killing and save my friends' lives.

Crazy?

What choice did I have?

I carried the old spellbook to my desk and, squinting in the dim light, quickly found the spell I'd been practicing. A Return spell.

Squeezing the jeweled bracelet in my hand, twisting it on my wrist, I mouthed the words of the spell once again.

I knew I needed to return . . . return to the Fear Mansion.

It was the only way to confront the murderers. The only place I knew I could find Angelica and Simon.

I shut my eyes tight and concentrated. I pictured the old mansion on top of its sloping, weed-choked hill. I pictured the brick turrets rising up on both sides like evil guardians.

"Return . . . return . . ."

Keeping my eyes shut tight, my muscles taut with concentration, I pictured Fear Street the way it used to be. Before the construction.

I pictured the gnarled, tangled old trees that covered both sides of the street, casting the whole neighborhood in darkness. In my mind I saw the Fear Street Woods: bramble bushes, all prickly, thorned shrubs, moss-stained trees tilting in every direction. And I pictured once again the old houses, the brick mansions built like forts.

And the most evil mansion of them all, the house of legends, of so much terror.

"Return . . . return . . ."

I had to go back there. I had to return to that house that no longer existed. To find that couple who *shouldn't* exist. The Fears who should have remained dead . . .

"Return . . . return . . ."

Spinning the bracelet in my hand, I kept my eyes shut and mouthed the ancient words. And I felt the cool silver grow warm. Yes. As I said the words, a tingling heat radiated from the bracelet, and the jewels glowed hot . . . hotter.

"Return . . . Yes, return . . ."

Could I make the Fear Mansion return?

I slid on my shoes, grabbed my down jacket, and tiptoed downstairs. Danny was snoring softly in his room. I stopped in the front entryway and swooped up the car keys.

No.

If I started the car, it would wake Mom

and Dad. I set the keys down and silently crept out the door, into the silence, the darkness, the coldness.

"Return . . . return . . ."

25

I walked the four blocks to Fear Street. A light rain had started to fall, a dewy mist, and it made the shrubs and lawns glisten. As if I'm walking through some sort of child's fairyland, I thought. Not heading to a house of evil.

I shuddered and pulled up the hood on my jacket.

As I crossed Powell, a family of raccoons darted out from under a hedge. Startled, I jumped back. There were four or five of them, all different sizes, and they shuffled across the street a few feet in front of me. I watched them disappear around the side of a house.

They're Night People too, I thought. All kinds of strange thoughts kept running through my head. I tried to force them away, to concentrate on my spells, on my . . . mission.

I turned onto Fear Street and heard the flapping of wings. Soft at first, then louder as the big bird swooped low over my head.

The one-eyed blackbird.

I ducked away from it. Buried my head in the parka hood.

The bird floated over me, staring at me with its one bulging black eye.

"Please—go away!" I tried to shout. But my plea came out in a choked whisper.

The frightening bird circled over me, once, twice, flying low. Was it going to attack?

No.

It turned in the air and swooped away, flapping its dark wings as it rose. It disappeared over the trees, flying over Fear Street.

I shivered. The cold mist covered my hot face. I brushed water from my eyes.

I suddenly thought of the burning owls, their wings outlined in bright yellow flames, screeching, screeching. And once again, I pictured the evil blackbird, its one eye staring so cold and cruel.

I squeezed the bracelet. It felt warm in my hand.

I took a deep breath and ran the rest of the way to Fear Street.

"Return . . . return . . ."

And yes, there it stood on its dark hill. The Fear Mansion had returned.

No lights from the shopping center. No familiar bar where we all met every night.

The old mansion loomed over me, sinister and menacing. And I knew I had no choice. I had to go inside and face the evil that awaited me there.

Rainwater ran down my face. My shoes sank into the marshy grass and mud as I made my way up the hill. An even deeper darkness washed over me as I stepped into the shadow of the house.

The front doors creaked open. And again, I felt the hard pressure at my back, the invisible force pushing me forward, pushing me into the house.

Did someone whisper my name?

Or was that the wind through the trees?

I stopped in the front entryway. I shook water off my coat and lowered the hood. I waited for my eyes to adjust to the dim light.

Pale yellow light seeped from a room down the front hall.

"Is anyone here?"

My shrill voice echoed against the bare walls.

Without realizing it, I was gripping the bracelet tightly. I let go of it, felt its warmth disappear, and started walking toward the light.

"Who is here?" I cried. "Is anyone here?"

The house creaked and groaned. My only reply.

I swallowed hard. My throat felt dry as sand. I tried to ignore the hard pounding of my heart.

"Is anyone here?"

The yellow light seeped over my shoes as I stopped outside the room. My legs started to tremble.

Why was there a light on inside this house? Someone had to be in that room.

I heard a rustling sound inside it. A soft scraping.

Gathering my courage, I gripped the door frame, stuck my head out slowly, and peeked into the room.

Bare walls. No furniture. The light filtered down from the ceiling.

Squinting hard, I saw a shadow move. No. Not a shadow.

The blackbird.

Standing on a slender wooden perch, it raised its wings and ducked its head as if greeting me.

How did it get in here?

Why was it here?

It kept its eye on me, staring back at me coldly, tilting its head from side to side. I cringed, seeing the empty eye socket, the black hole in the side of the bird's head.

And then, without warning, it took off. Pushed itself from its perch and darted toward me, raising its talons and screeching its attack call.

"No—!" I tried to dodge away. But the bird fastened its claws around my shoulders. Beating its wings in my face, it lowered its open beak and—

—and I heard a shout.

I saw an arm swing. A hand slapped the side of the bird, slapped it hard.

Stunned, the big bird fell back. Screeching in anger, it raised its wings, floated back . . . back onto its perch. Bobbing, it squinted at me with its one eye.

I turned to see who had rescued me. A figure moved into the pale light, raised his face to me—and I let out a shocked scream.

"*You?* What are *you* doing here?"

26

Lewis wrapped his arms around me, a strange smile on his face. "I followed you," he said. "I came to help you. I guess I arrived just in time."

My breath caught in my throat. I grabbed his hands. They were cold as ice.

"I . . . I'm so glad to see you," I said. "That bird—it wanted to kill me. But—how did you know? I—"

"I was on my way to your house," he said. "I saw you leave. I followed you here. I knew you'd need my help."

On its perch, the bird flapped its wings and let out a shrill squawk.

I grabbed Lewis. "That awful bird. Why—?"

"Jamie, follow me," Lewis whispered.

I hesitated. He took my hand and pulled

me to the hall. "Where?" I cried. "Where are you taking me?"

He guided me down the dark, narrow hall. The air grew colder as we walked.

"We have to end this," he said softly, holding on to me.

"Yes," I agreed. "That's why I came, Lewis. But—where are we going?"

"It's time to end it," he repeated, lowering his voice nearly to a growl.

We turned a corner. Again, yellow light washed into the hallway from a room near the far end.

Lewis kept his eyes straight ahead. He gripped my wrist in his icy hand. His features were taut, tight with worry—or fear.

I didn't understand. My mind spun with questions.

Where was he taking me? Why didn't I hear him following me here? Why wasn't he surprised that the Fear Mansion was back?

He started walking faster, pushing me toward the yellow light.

"Lewis? Stop," I said. "You're scaring me. Can't you explain what's going on?"

"You'll see," he said, avoiding my eyes. "Don't you trust me, Jamie? I just saved your life."

Trust him? Of course. I trusted him more than anyone else on earth. But why was he acting so strangely?

He brought his face close to mine. I could feel his hot breath on my cheek. He whispered, "It's time."

He guided me into a large room—dark walls, bare wood floors, no furniture, the pale light washing down from the ceiling.

I blinked. People came rushing toward me. Too fast. It was all happening too fast.

I saw Dana, Shark, and Nate. They looked eerily pale in the yellow light. Sick. Their faces tight with fear, eyes wide, all talking at once.

"What are you doing here?" I shouted. "How did you get here?"

The blackbird fluttered over my head. It swooped into the room and perched on a windowsill.

Dana grabbed my hand. "I don't like this, Jamie," she said, her voice cracking. "What is happening? Do you know?"

"How do we get out of here?" Shark demanded.

"Yeah. We want out of here," Nate agreed. "Jamie, what's going on? Can we leave now?"

I felt Lewis step up behind me. He bumped me and grabbed my elbow. "Jamie will help you out," he told them. "No problem. Jamie will show you the way out."

"Huh? Lewis? What are you talking about?" I cried. "Enough already. Stop being so mysterious and—"

My breath caught in my throat when I saw his eyes.

Pale eyes. Silvery and cold. Not Lewis's eyes. I knew Lewis's eyes.

I gasped as I figured it out. A sudden flash and I knew. Staring into those *wrong* eyes, I knew the truth.

"You . . . you're not Lewis!" I choked out.

He snickered. His face filled with amusement. "It took you so long, Jamie."

The others shrank back, staring in silence. Had they figured it out too?

Lewis gripped my arm, holding me in place. "No, I'm not your friend Lewis," he said.

"I think you've guessed. I'm Simon Fear."

"I . . . I trusted you," I choked out. "I confided in you. And all the time . . ." My fear tightened my throat, choked off my words.

All these weeks, I'd been searching for Angelica Fear. Afraid that Angelica was nearby, afraid that she would possess me again.

But Angelica was gone. Destroyed. Back in her grave somewhere. And all the while, Simon Fear had been the one, the one who had murdered my friends, the one I should have been afraid of.

Lewis. So close to me. The evil had been so close. . . .

Simon motioned to Dana, Shark, and Nate. "Welcome to my home. Or, should I say, welcome *back*."

His face changed quickly, like those stopmotion science movies. He aged in seconds. He flashed me a tight-lipped smile, a cruel, cold smile.

"I escaped my grave the same night my wife, Angelica, escaped hers," he said. "Jamie, you and your friend Lewis had the honor of awakening us. You fell on our graves. You made it so easy for us. You gave us new bodies."

My friends gasped.

I tried to step away from Simon Fear, but he kept his grip on my arm.

"Let us out of here!" Shark demanded. "You're crazy!"

"Please—let us go!" Nate pleaded.

Simon's smile faded. "You didn't mind being here last year," he said with a sneer. "You didn't mind coming into our house and looting our treasures, our precious possessions, taking whatever pleased you."

"Just let us go!" Dana cried. "You're crazy! I wasn't even here then."

Simon's face reddened with rage. "*You're* the one who murdered Angelica!" he screamed.

Dana gasped. She raised her hands to her mouth and staggered back against the wall.

Simon stared at us, breathing hard now. "Here you are, in my house. Back where you committed your crime. Your *fatal* crime."

"But, please—," I started.

"Don't you see?" he continued, ignoring me. "The others have all been punished. You are the only ones left. The only ones who still have to die."

We stared at him in silence.

I felt my pulse start to race. My throat tightened until I could barely breathe.

On its windowsill perch, the blackbird squawked and flapped its wings excitedly.

Nate spoke up first in a trembling voice. "We'll return the stuff," he said. "Is that what you want? Want us to return your stuff?"

"Too late," Simon replied through clenched teeth. "I'm afraid it's too late."

Shark took a few steps forward. He stared hard at Simon, challenging him. "You just said Jamie would show us the way out."

Simon tossed back his head and laughed. "She will. She will," he said.

He shoved me toward them. "I'll keep my word. Jamie will show you out," he repeated. "You see, *she's* the one who is going to kill you."

27

"No way!" I screamed. "You can't force me to do anything against my friends. You can't—"

He reached under his jacket and pulled out a silvery object. The amulet! He pushed it toward me, his gray eyes locked coldly on mine.

"Jamie, you have no say. You have no power to fight me. I have the amulet." He raised it higher. The blue jewels glowed under the yellow light from above.

"I became the blackbird," he said. "Sometimes your friend Lewis's dull body was too confining. Some nights, I transformed into this poor, one-eyed bird and rode the night sky."

The glow of the amulet burned my eyes. I turned my head away.

"You murdered Angelica," Simon said, his face reddening once again, revealing his anger. "But I flew into your garage and grabbed the amulet."

He sighed. "When Angelica and I returned to life last year, we planned to live together forever. But you destroyed that plan by murdering my beloved wife. Ever since, I've been planning what I should do with you, Jamie. For yours will be a special fate."

I backed away. "You—you're going to kill me?"

He shook his head. "No. Death is not for you. Death would be too simple. I'm going to keep you with me, Jamie. At my side. You will live forever—as Angelica. You and I will live together forever, and you will do my bidding."

I gasped. "Your bidding?"

He nodded. He pulled the amulet from around his neck and stepped toward me. "You will put this on now. The amulet will guide you. The amulet will show you how to end your friends' lives. So we may begin our eternal quest."

My friends stared in horror as he raised the

chain and started to slip the amulet over my head. At the windowsill, I heard the bird squawk. I heard Shark yell, "Jamie—run!"

But I didn't run. I'd waited too long for this confrontation.

I shoved Simon back and raised my arm. My sleeve dropped, and he saw the silver, jeweled bracelet.

"Simon, I've learned my own spells!" I cried in a voice quivering with emotion. "I'm the one who returned the Fear Mansion to its hill tonight. I did that. And now I'm going to use this bracelet for another spell I learned. I'm going to return you to your grave!"

Simon narrowed his eerie, gunmetal eyes at me. The amulet trembled in his hands.

Holding the bracelet up to him, I began to chant the words of the chant I'd memorized.

"Return . . . return . . ."

I waved the bracelet in a circle.

"Return . . . return . . ."

Would the spell work?

Still chanting, I raised my eyes.

Why was Simon Fear laughing at me?

28

With a groan, I lowered the bracelet.
I suddenly felt weary, weak. Helpless.

Gripping the amulet in both hands, Simon grinned at me. "Did you honestly think *you* returned my home to Fear Street tonight? Poor, naive Jamie. The sad truth is, that bracelet is powerless in your hands."

His smile faded. His mouth formed an angry scowl. "I returned my home tonight," he growled. "I set the trap for you all. I'm the only one who can use the power of Angelica's bracelet. Jamie, I used the bracelet to strengthen my power over you. I used it to bring you here tonight."

"No—!" I cried. "I can feel its power. You didn't—"

He silenced me with a wave of his hand.

"Why do you think I stole it for you? When you wear the bracelet, you are a prisoner of my will."

I tried to steady my breathing. I suddenly felt as if my chest would burst.

Were the spells I'd carefully taught myself really useless?

I shuddered. The bracelet—it suddenly went cold. The cold penetrated my wrist until I gasped in pain.

"Go!" I motioned to Dana, Nate, and Shark. "Run! I can't help you! Just run!"

They gazed at me in shock.

"We can't leave you here!" Dana cried.

"Go!" I shouted, waving frantically. "Go! Hurry!"

They hesitated another second, then took off, scrambling toward the hall.

My arm went up. Against my will, I raised my hand, the hand with the bracelet. The freezing cold bracelet tingled my wrist. And as I raised it high, my friends stopped.

They froze.

Froze in place and didn't move.

I stared at their horrified, open-mouthed faces.

Simon grabbed my hand and lowered it to my side. He wrapped his hand around the bracelet, and I felt another sharp tingle, like an electrical shock.

"Good work, Jamie." His hot breath brushed my ear. "Or should I start to call you Angelica?"

"N-no—," I stammered.

"Good work," he repeated. "You stopped your friends from escaping. See how easy that was?"

"Simon, please—," I begged. I couldn't move, either. Had he frozen me, too?

He slipped the amulet over my neck and arranged it carefully over my throat. "Now, follow the amulet's will, Angelica's will," he whispered. His cheek brushed mine and sent chills down my body. "Follow the amulet's will, Jamie. Use it to kill all three of them. Then you and I will begin our journey together."

"Yes, Simon," I said softly, staring blankly straight ahead. The room was a blur, except for the black figure of the bird in the window.

"Yes, Simon," I repeated. "I will do the amulet's bidding."

I gripped the amulet—the metal so hot between my hands—and began to chant the ancient words.

29

The amulet glowed in my hands. Its warmth flowed through my body.

My friends didn't move. I glimpsed them, frozen in place, all three faces revealing their terror.

Gripping the amulet tightly, I continued to chant.

"STOP!"

Simon's shrill cry echoed off the bare walls.

I raised my eyes to him and saw him gripping the sides of his head with both hands. "STOP!" he screamed. "What are you doing? What are you doing to me?"

I shoved the amulet toward him and, ignoring his command, continued to chant.

He doubled over in pain. He gripped his stomach. Dropped to the floor on his knees.

"Stop! Stop it! I know what you're doing!"

I finished the spell. "I learned more than one spell," I told him, watching him twist in agony on the floor. "I studied that book a lot, Simon. I taught myself a lot."

"Stop it! Please—"

"And now I have the power of the amulet," I said, holding it over him. "Thank you for that, Simon. Thank you for giving me the power to destroy you."

"No—" He struggled to his feet. He made a grab for the amulet.

I jerked it from his hand.

"Too weak . . . ," he groaned. He dropped back to his knees.

"Good-bye, Simon," I said. I started to chant some more. The amulet glowed brighter. Its warmth swept down my arm, down my body.

"You . . . can't . . . hold . . . me," he whispered. His body sank facedown on the floor.

Still mouthing the words, I stared down at him. And saw the green smoke starting to pour from his ears. Thick as pea soup, it rose up toward the ceiling. A dark green gas, twisting, curling as it rose.

I stopped my chant and watched it float across the room toward the blackbird on the window. "I know what you're doing!" I screamed.

The green gas—it was Simon's spirit. He was escaping Lewis's body—and moving into the blackbird.

The bird flapped its wings. It tilted its head back, its one eye glowing, as the green gas began to pour into its gaping eye socket.

Simon is escaping, I realized.

I watched the thick green gas pour into the bird. The bird arched its back as the gas vanished into the hole in the side of its head. Then it raised its wings and let out a fierce cry that rang in my ears.

I had no time to move.

It leaped off the windowsill, soared to the ceiling. Raised its talons and once again came swooping down at me, screeching at the top of its lungs.

I ducked and dropped to the floor. The talons ripped at my hair, scratched the top of my head.

Pain shot down my head, my neck. I spun

around as the bird raised itself, preparing to attack again.

I raised the amulet and shouted out the words of another spell I'd memorized. Shouted in a shrill, hoarse voice, waving the amulet toward the bird.

The last spell I knew. The last one.

Would it work?

The blackbird appeared to freeze in midair. Its screeches ended in a whelp of pain. It turned toward the window. Flapping hard, it flew a few feet—

—and then a deafening explosion rocked the room.

I ducked and covered my face as the black-bird exploded.

Feathers came floating down in a blizzard of black.

Wet bird guts smacked my forehead. I saw the bird's one eye bounce over the floor. Its eyeless head plopped at my side.

I jumped to my feet. I knew I had to res-cue Dana, Shark, and Nate.

I brushed black feathers and hot bird guts from my hair. I started to raise the amulet toward my friends—and it slipped from my hands.

It hit the floor in front of my feet, bounced away—and the room started to shake.

I heard a thunderlike rumble. Boards cracking. I saw the walls split. The floor shook. The rumble grew into a roar.

The house is coming down, I realized.

It's all coming down.

We're trapped in here. We're all going to die!

30

I made a grab for the amulet. Missed.

Darkness washed over me, a deeper darkness than I'd ever seen before. I couldn't tell if my eyes were open or shut.

How much time passed? I couldn't tell. It may have been only a second or two. It may have been longer.

Focus. Focus . . . The blur of shadows and lights finally sharpened, and I saw that I was standing on a sidewalk.

Lights blinked in front of me. The familiar red and green of a traffic light. And behind it, the lights of the Fear Street Acres shopping center.

"Hey, Jamie—?"

I spun around and saw Lewis. He blinked at me, shaking his head groggily. Dana, Nate, and Shark stood against the brick wall of the bar. Nights Bar.

We all gazed at one another as if seeing one another for the first time.

I felt totally clear, refreshed. The evil had been washed away. Simon, Angelica, the old house . . . their evil gone. The whole world seemed lighter, brighter—even in the middle of the night.

I took a deep breath of the cold night air. I suddenly felt so happy. I grabbed Lewis's arm.

"Hi," he said, almost shyly. "Can you tell me what just happened?"

"Why are we standing outside the bar in the cold?" Shark asked.

Nate glanced around tensely. "I don't remember coming here," he said. "Weird."

"Yeah. Weird," I murmured.

"Did we all drive together?" Dana asked.

They didn't remember anything about tonight.

Fine, I thought. I'm not going to fill them in. They probably wouldn't believe it, anyway.

We started into the bar. I stopped at the doorway.

Hey, I left the amulet in the mansion, I thought. Where is it now?

Better forget it, Jamie, I decided. Let it stay buried with all its evil.

I followed the others into Nights. I waved to Ryland O'Connor and started toward our usual table in the back.

"Hey—stop. Aren't you forgetting something?" Ryland asked. "Kiss the plaque for good luck."

I turned and stared at Simon and Angelica on the brass plaque. Then I turned back to Ryland.

"I don't think so," I said.

About the Author

R.L. Stine invented the teen horror genre with Fear Street, the bestselling teen horror series of all time. He also changed the face of children's publishing with the mega-successful Goosebumps series, which *Guinness World Records* cites as the Best-Selling Children's Books ever, and went on to become a world-wide multimedia phenomenon. The first two books in his new series Mostly Ghostly, *Who Let the Ghosts Out?* and *Have You Met My Ghoulfriend?* are *New York Times* bestsellers. He's thrilled to be writing for teens again in the brand-new Fear Street Nights books.

R.L. Stine has received numerous awards of recognition, including several Nickelodeon Kids' Choice Awards and Disney Adventures Kids' Choice Awards, and he has been selected by kids as one of their favorite authors in the National Education Association Read Across America. He lives in New York City with his wife, Jane, and their dog, Nadine.

DON'T MISS A SINGLE NIGHT

It all started with Lewis and Jamie. They were sneaking out late at night to be together. Then their friends started joining in. First at the old burnt-down Fear Mansion. Later, at the local bar Nights.

They called themselves the Night People. And they carefully protected their secret world. No parents, no work, no stress. Just chilling with friends in their own private after hours club.

But then the nights turned dark. Unexplainable accidents, evil pranks . . . and then, later, the killings. The Night People know they have to stop the horror all by themselves, or else they risk exposure. Not to mention their lives.

ISBN 1-416-904123